A New Brain

music and lyrics by

William Finn

book by

William Finn & James Lapine

New York Hollywood London Toronto

SAMUELFRENCH.COM

CAUTION: Professionals and amateurs are hereby warned that *A NEW BRAIN*, being fully protected under the copyright laws of the United States of America, the British Commonwealth, including Canada, and the other countries of the Copyright Union, is subject to a royalty, and anyone presenting the play without the consent of the owners or their authorized agents will be liable to the penalties by law provided.

Amateurs wishing to arrange for the production of *A NEW BRAIN*, must make application to SAMUEL FRENCH, INC., at 45 West 25th Street, New York, NY 10010-2751, giving the following particulars:

(1) The name of the town and theatre or hall in which the proposed production will be presented.

(2) The maximum seating capacity of the theatre or hall.

(3) Scale of ticket prices; and

(4) The number of performances intended and the dates thereof.

Upon receipt of these particulars SAMUEL FRENCH, INC., will quote the amateur terms and availability.

Stock royalty and availability quoted on application to SAMUEL FRENCH, INC., at 45 West 25th Street, New York, NY 10010-2751.

For all other rights than those stipulated above, apply to William Morris Agency, 1325 Avenue of the Americas, New York, NY 10019.

An orchestration consisting of **piano/conductor's score, synthesizer, drums/percussion, reed (alto saxophone, clarinet, oboe), french horn and Cello** will be loaned two months prior to the production ONLY on receipt of the royalty quoted for all performances, the rental fee and a refundable deposit. The deposit will be refunded on the safe return to SAMUEL FRENCH, INC. of all materials loaned for the production.

ISBN 978-0-573-62713-2 Printed in U.S.A #16593

IMPORTANT BILLING AND CREDIT REQUIREMENTS

All producers of A NEW BRAIN *must* give credit to the Authors of the Work in all programs distributed in connection with performances of the Work, and in all instances in which the title of the Work appears for the purposes of advertising, publicizing or otherwise exploiting a production thereof, including, without limitation, programs, souvenir books and playbills. The names of the Authors must appear on a separate line in which no other matter appears, immediately following the title of the Work, and *must* be in size of type not less than 50% of the size used for the title of the Work.

Billing *must* be substantially as follows:

(NAME OF PRODUCER)

Presents

A NEW BRAIN

Music and Lyrics by
William Finn

Book by
William Finn and James Lapine

The following *must* also be included in any programs distributed in connection with performances of the Work:

Originally produced by Lincoln Center Theatre,
New York City

Vocal Arrangements by Jason Robert Brown

LINCOLN CENTER THEATER AT THE MITZI E. NEWHOUSE

under the direction of

André Bishop and Bernard Gersten

presents

A NEW BRAIN

music and lyrics by
William Finn

book by
William Finn & James Lapine

with (in alphabetical order)

Kristin Chenoweth
Penny Fuller
Malcolm Gets
John Jellison
Keith Byron Kirk
Liz Larsen
Norm Lewis
Michael Mandell
Mary Testa
Chip Zien

sets
David Gallo

costumes
Toni-Leslie James

lighting
Peggy Eisenhauer

sound
Tony Meola

orchestrations
Michael Starobin

music director/additional vocal arrangements
Ted Sperling

vocal arrangements
Jason Robert Brown

casting
Alan Filderman

stage manager
Bonnie Panson

musical theater associate producer
Ira Weitzman

director of marketing & special projects
Thomas Cott

director of development
Hattie K. Jutagir

general manager
Steven C. Callahan

production manager
Jeff Hamlin

directed and choreographed by
Graciela Daniele

CHARACTERS
(in order of appearance)

GORDON MICHAEL SCHWINN

A HOMELESS LADY

RHODA

WAITRESS

MR. BUNGEE

RICHARD, the nice nurse

NANCY D., the thin nurse

DR. JAFAR BERENSTEINER

THE MINISTER

ROGER DELLI-BOVI

MIMI SCHWINN, the mother

A NOTE ABOUT THE SET DESIGN

Let me try to describe David Gallo's fabulous set for Graciela Daniele's wonderful production:

It's basically a room, a hospital room — with a large window on the back wall into which panoramas of the street and various other things are slotted. There are kooky streamlined chairs, travelling hospital curtains which appear and disappear, an MRI (looking like a large tomb) and a bed.

The lighting, as devised by Peggy Eisenhauer, was expressionistic and dramatic, and should so be when produced elsewhere.

William Finn

MUSICAL NUMBERS

PROLOGUE

FROGS HAVE SO MUCH SPRING ("THE SPRING SONG")
CALAMARI
911 EMERGENCY/I HAVE SO MANY SONGS

HEART AND MUSIC
TROUBLE IN HIS BRAIN
MOTHER'S GONNA MAKE THINGS FINE
BE POLITE TO EVERYONE
I'D RATHER BE SAILING
FAMILY HISTORY
GORDO'S LAW OF GENETICS
AND THEY'RE OFF
ROGER ARRIVES
JUST GO
POOR, UNSUCCESSFUL AND FAT
OPERATION TOMORROW
SITTING BECALMED IN THE LEE OF CUTTYHUNK
CRANIOTOMY
AN INVITATION TO SLEEP IN MY ARMS
CHANGE
YES
IN THE MIDDLE OF THE ROOM (PART 1)
THROW IT OUT
IN THE MIDDLE OF THE ROOM (PART 2)
A REALLY LOUSY DAY IN THE UNIVERSE
BRAIN DEAD
WHENEVER I DREAM
EATING MYSELF UP ALIVE
THE MUSIC STILL PLAYS ON
DON'T GIVE IN
YOU BOYS ARE GONNA GET ME IN SUCH TROUBLE/I'D RATHER BE SAILING *(REPRISE)*
THE HOMELESS LADY'S REVENGE
TIME
I FEEL SO MUCH SPRING

PROLOGUE

(In the REAR WINDOW is a smaller window in a wall with a wall clock. On the ledge of the window are piles of books.

Lights up on GORDON working at the piano.)

GORDON.
FROGS HAVE SO MUCH SPRING WITHIN THEM.
JUMP, FROG, JUMP,
JUMP SO HIGH YOU SPLIT YOUR TIGHTS.
(To himself.) That bites. That bites. *(He scratches out some lyrics on his notepad. Sings as if he's making the lyrics up on the spot.)*
FROGS HAVE SO MUCH SPRING WITHIN THEM,
JUMP, FROG, JUMP,
LILY PADS ARE YOUR NEXT STOP — *(Thinks.)*
KERPLOP — *(Thinks.)*
YOU MISSED THE LILY PAD. *(Screams.)*
WHAT THE HELL AM I DOING?
WHO'M I FOOLING?
WRITING SONGS FOR FRO-O-OGS.
THOSE NASTY GNATS.
THEY'RE NATURE'S LITTLE ACROBATS
I HATE THEM MORE THAN KITTY CATS.
Ugh. *(Just sings anything. Stops playing, fairly disgusted at this inane song. A clock chime goes off, ringing twice.)* Lunch with Rhoda! To be continued.

(GORDON exits.
A HOMELESS WOMAN enters from right. GORDON crosses her on his way to lunch.)

HOMELESS WOMAN *(To GORDON)*
HEY, MISTER. *(To audience)*
PENNIES OR NICKELS OR DIMES.
WE LIVE IN PERILOUS TIMES.

HOMELESS WOMAN. Could you spare some change?

GORDON. Sorry, not today.
HOMELESS WOMAN. If not today, when?
PENNIES OR NICKELS OR DIMES.

(HOMELESS WOMAN exits. REAR WINDOW: ferns. GORDON arrives at a restaurant table where he greets his best friend RHODA.)

GORDON.
SORRY I'M LATE, RHODA.
RHODA. Ach, you're always late.
GORDON.
I WAS WORKING ON THE "SPRING SONG."
IS HE ANGRY
THAT HE DOESN'T HAVE
THE "SPRING SONG" YET?
I BET.
RHODA.
NO, HE'S ANGRY THAT HE DOESN'T HAVE THE "YES SONG."
GORDON.
I HATE THE "YES SONG."
I HATE THE "SPRING SONG."
I HATE MR. BUNGEE AND THIS JOB.
IT'S SO SAD
WORKING ON MR. BUNGEE'S LILY PAD.

(The WAITRESS had entered earlier and heard the whole conversation.)

WAITRESS. You work for Mr. Bungee? I love that show!
THE SPECIALS TODAY
THOUGH NOT MANY,
ARE ESPECIALLY GOOD.
FIRST THE FISH OF THE DAY:
CALAMARI
WHICH ISN'T A FISH
BUT LIVES IN THE SEA,
AS SET IN THE DISH
IT HAPPENS TO BE
THE FISH OF THE DAY.
Okay.
PLUS THERE'S THE ZITI
WITH A SAUCE THAT'S MEATY.
IT'S FUN —
GORDON and RHODA. *(Amused by nothing.)* Fun.

WAITRESS.
AND THERE'S A LOT
AND THAT'S THE SPECIALS.
(As if she had just auditioned.) Thank you.

GORDON. Well, I'll have the ziti and a diet coke.

RHODA. And I'll have the goat cheese salad — no cheese.

GORDON. Yeah, yeah. Thank you.

RHODA. So what's going on with you anyway?

GORDON.
HE'S TAKING UP THE BRUNT OF MY TIME.

RHODA. It's called a job.

GORDON.
I DON'T HAVE TIME TO WRITE MY REAL STUFF.
BUT I FEEL STUFF ...

RHODA.
YOU'RE A MESS!

GORDON.
I CAN'T EXPRESS
WHAT I MEAN TO CONVEY.
SO, OF COURSE, I DIDN'T
WRITE ENOUGH TODAY.

RHODA.
IF YOU DON'T KEEP WRITING
YOU'LL BE SHOWN THE DOOR
YOU KNOW MR. BUNGEE HATES YOU.

GORDON.
I HATE MR. BUNGEE.

RHODA.
I THINK HE HATES YOU MORE.

GORDON.
WHY DOES MR. BUNGEE HATE ME?

RHODA.
FIRST OFF,
YOU'VE GOTTA FINISH A SONG.
YOU SCOFF.
BUT DAMMIT WRITE THE "SPRING SONG."
WRITE THE "YES SONG."
DON'T LET YOU CAREER
GO TO THE DOGS.

GORDON.
AS YOU CAN TELL
I DON'T WRITE WELL
FOR FROGS.

(Enter MR. BUNGEE dressed as a giant frog, which is what he plays on the television show.)

GORDON. Oh, my God, Rhoda. I feel like I'm having hallucinations.
RHODA. What are you talking about?
GORDON. He's not here right now, is he?
MR. BUNGEE.
MR. BUNGEE IS AQUATIC.
AND DESPOTIC.
MR. BUNGEE'S OCEANIC.
AND SATANIC.
MR. BUNGEE'S SAID TO BE TYRANNICAL AT TIMES.
AND MR. BUNGEE ALWAYS RHYMES.
WAITRESS. *(Carrying their order)*
I LOVE MR. BUNGEE.
YES INDEEDEE.
HERE'S YOUR ZITI.
I LOVE MR. BUNGEE WHEN HE
MAKES HIS SCENES.

MR. BUNGEE. Whee!

I LOVE MR. BUN—
DID SOMEONE ORDER SCALOPPINI?
I LOVE MR. BUNGEE.
HERE'S YOUR DIET COKE.
AND HERE'S YOUR GREENS.
(Quietly she exits.)
I LOVE MR. BUNGEE.
I LOVE MR. BUNGEE.
RHODA.
FIRST WRITE YOU SONG, THEN NEXT
YOU'LL WRITE THE EPIC

MR. BUNGEE. Oh, sure.

FIRST, KID'S TV, THEN NEXT
BROADWAY SHOWS.

MR. BUNGEE. Ha!

IT'S A ROCKY ROAD FROM LILY PAD
TO WHERE YOU WANT TO GET TO, DEAR,
BUT RHODA ALWAYS KNOWS.

MR. BUNGEE. Him? A Broadway show? I don't think so!

(MR. BUNGEE exits.)

GORDON.
INSIDE ME I FEEL WASHED UP AND THROUGH.

RHODA. Oh, come on, Gordon.
GORDON.
WRITING THIS SHIT'S KILLED MY TALENT.
RHODA. That's not true.
GORDON.
AND WHATEVER'S LEFT TO KILL
THEN BUNGEE WILL
GRIND THAT DOWN TO SQUAT.
I USED TO BE —
RHODA.
YOU'RE STILL —
GORDON.
I WAS —
RHODA.
I DON'T AGREE.
GORDON.
I ONCE WAS — BUT I'M NOT!
RHODA. Hey.
GORDON. NOT, I tell you.
RHODA. Hey, sit down.
GORDON. Oh my — *(GORDON is holding his head.)*
SOMETHING IS WRONG.
RHODA. Gordon, are you okay?
GORDON.
SOMETHING IS WRONG.
RHODA. Gordon, you're scaring me.
GORDON. Something is very, very, very wrong.

(He falls face first into the food.)

RHODA. Gordon! Gordon!

(A stretcher is wheeled in by HOSPITAL STAFF. During this, DOCTORS may do a sternum rub as they call his name, look into his eyes, check his blood pressure, check for stiff neck, an EKG, a CAT scan.)

HOSPITAL STAFF.
911 EMERGENCY
TAKE HIM DOWN TO NYU.
STROKE'S A POSSIBILITY.
RHODA. *(Trying not to be hysterical)*
I SHOULD TRY TO LOCATE ROGER.
DOCTOR.
LIFT HIM CAREF'LLY ON ONE-TWO-THREE.

ALL.
AND UP!

(They lift him up.)

RICHARD.
CHECK THE PULSE AND WATCH HIS EYES.
NANCY D.
CALL THE DEPARTMENT OF NEUROLOGY.
RHODA.
I SHOULD TRY TO LOCATE HIS MOTHER.
ALL.
SOMEBODY TRY TO LOCATE HIS MOTHER!

RICHARD.
WHEN WAS HE LAST SEEN EATING?
RHODA. *(Dissembling, crying)*
I DON'T KNOW.
NANCY D.
HYSTERICS ARE SELF DEFEATING.
DONTCHA KNOW?
DOCTOR.
PRESENCE OF BLEEDING.
ALL.
WHERE THIS . .
DOCTOR.
WHOLE MESS IS LEADING . . .
ALL.
WE CANNOT SAY FOR SURE YET.
MINISTER.
IS THE IV SECURE YET?
RHODA.
ROGER'S SAILING NEAR MARTHA'S VINEYARD.

NANCY D. Patient's name?

RHODA. Gordon Schwinn.

NANCY D. Are you next of kin?

RHODA. I wish. We work together. He's gay.

NANCY D. Is he HIV?

RHODA. I can't be absolutely sure but I don't think so. No. The answer is no. I think.

(Singing begins again.)

NANCY D.
FIRST THE BLOOD TESTS
THEN EKG.

STAFF.
AND THEN:
NANCY D.
GET A CAT SCAN, WATCH HIS EYES.
STAFF.
AND THEN:
NANCY D.
CALL THE DEPARTMENT OF NEUROLOGY.
RHODA.
I SHOULD TRY TO CANCEL MY THERAPY.
STAFF.
AND THEN:
RHODA.
I SHOULD GET IN TOUCH WITH HIS MOTHER.
STAFF.
AND THEN:
RHODA.
I SHOULD TRY TO LOCATE ROGER.

(As they are working on a body the audience thinks is GORDON, GORDON emerges from behind the closed medical screens.)

GORDON.
ALL THE SONGS I NEVER WROTE
FIZZLE AND REMAIN.
ALL THE SONGS I DID NOT START.
ALL THE RHYMES I NEVER MADE.
ALL THE STORIES I DELAYED
IN TELLING
ARE WELLING UP
INSIDE MY BRAIN.
I SHOULD EXPLAIN
I HAVE SO MANY SONGS.
I HAVE SO MANY SONGS.
I HAVE SO MANY SONGS.

HEART AND MUSIC

	MINISTER.
	STORIES OF PASSION STORIES OF FRIENDSHIP AND TALES OF HOW RO- MANCE SURVIVES
GORDON.	
I HAVE SO MANY SONGS	
	STORIES OF "YES"ES, OF FROGS MAKING MESSES AND POOR, UNSUCCESSFUL, AND FAT PEOPLE'S LIVES
STORIES OF LIVING	
	STORIES OF LIVING
STORIES OF DYING	
	STORIES OF DYING
AND WAYS WE CAN DEAL WITH OUR FEAR	AND WAYS WE CAN DEAL WITH OUR FEAR
	RHODA and HOMELESS WOMAN.
	OH — OH
STORIES OF HORSES PARENTAL DIVORCES	
AND HOW RICH OR POOR	OH —
IT'S A VERY SMALL SPHERE	OH —
WHERE WE APPEAR.	OH —
BUT YOU GOTTA HAVE	AH!
HEART AND MUSIC YOU GOTTA HAVE HEART AND MUSIC GET ALONG	
GORDON.	**RHODA, MINISTER HOMELESS WOMAN, MOTHER, ROGER.**
YOU GOTTA HAVE HEART AND MUSIC YOU GOTTA HAVE	YOU GOTTA HAVE HEART AND MUSIC YOU GOTTA HAVE

HEART AND MUSIC	HEART AND MUSIC
HEART AND MUSIC MAKE A SONG.	HEART AND MUSIC MAKE A SONG.
	ALL.
IF I ONLY HAD THE TIME	OH — OH
WHAT I WOULD WRITE	
FOR YOUR DELIGHT	OH — AH — AH —
	ROGER.
	STORIES OF ILLNESS
STORIES OF ILLNESS	
	SONGS OF IMPROVING
SONGS OF IMPROVING	**ALL.**
AND EVERYONE TALKS ABOUT CHANGE.	AND EVERYONE TALKS ABOUT CHANGE.
I HAVE SO MANY SONGS	
	STORIES OF STILLNESS
	OF PEOPLE NOT MOVING
AND THROWING OUT BOOKS	
WHEN THINGS TURN OUT TOO STRANGE.	
WE RE-ARRANGE.	
	ALL.
BUT WE GOTTA HAVE	BUT YA GOTTA HAVE
HEART AND	
	MUSIC
	YOU GOTTA HAVE
	HEART AND
MUSIC	
HEART AND MUSIC GET ALONG	HEART AND MUSIC GET ALONG
GORDON, ROGER, MOTHER, RICHARD, DOCTOR.	**RHODA, NANCY, HOMELESS WOMAN, MINISTER.**
	YOU GOTTA HAVE HEART AND MUSIC
YA GOTTA HAVE	
HEART AND MUSIC	HEART —
YOU GOTTA HAVE	
HEART AND MUSIC	HEART AND MUSIC
HEART AND MUSIC MAKE A SONG	HEART AND MUSIC MAKE A SONG
OH YA GOTTA HAVE	OH YA GOTTA HAVE

DOCTOR & RICHARD.	GORDON, MOTHER, ROGER.	HW and MINISTER.	RHODA and NANCY.
HEART.	HEART	HEART	HEART
EV'RYBODY	AND MUSIC	HEART AND MUSIC	YOU GOTTA HAVE HEART
GOTTA HAVE	YA GOTTA HAVE		
HEART AND MUSIC	HEART AND MUSIC	HEART AND MUSIC	
YA GOTTA HAVE			
HEART AND			
MUSIC	HEART AND MUSIC	YA GOTTA HAVE	HEART
OR YOU'RE NEVER	GET ALONG	SOME HEART	
GONNA GET ALONG		AND MUSIC	YOU'LL ALWAYS GET
NO NO NO NO NO	OH YOU GOTTA	YEAH YEAH YEAH	ALONG WITH YOUR
HAVE			HEART AND MUSIC
HEART EV'RYBODY	HEART AND MUSIC	HEART AND MUSIC	HEART
GOTTA HAVE	YA GOTTA HAVE	HEART AND MUSIC	YA GOTTA HAVE HEART
HEART AND MUSIC	HEART AND MUSIC		
YA GOTTA HAVE			
HEART AND			HEART
MUSIC	HEART AND MUSIC	YA GOTTA HAVE	
HEART AND MUSIC	MAKE A SONG	SOME HEART AND MUSIC	YOU'LL ALWAYS GET ALONG WITH YOUR
CAN MAKE A SONG			
		YEAH	HEART AND MUSIC

ALL.
YOU'LL ALWAYS GET ALONG WITH YOUR HEART
WITH YOUR HEART
WITH YOUR HEART ... AND MUSIC

GORDON.
HEART AND MUSIC MAKE

ALL.
HEART AND MUSIC MAKE
HEART AND MUSIC MAKE

GORDON.
MAKE A SONG!

MEN.	LADIES.
HEART AND MUSIC	HEART AND MUSIC

MEN.	LADIES.
MAKE A SONG	MAKE A SONG ...
HEART AND MUSIC	
MAKE A SONG	
HEART AND MUSIC	HEART AND MUSIC
MAKE A SONG!	MAKE A SONG!

TROUBLE IN HIS BRAIN

(The tempo starts out slowly.)

DOCTOR.
BRAIN
MOTHER.
BRAIN
DOCTOR.
THERE'S TROUBLE IN HIS BRAIN.
ANEURYSM, TUMOR — WE DON'T KNOW.
CAT SCAN TOLD US
LOTS OF FLUID
SITS AROUND THE BRAIN.
AND SO
WE MUST OPERATE.

DRAIN
MOTHER.
DRAIN?
DOCTOR.
GOTTA DRAIN THE BRAIN.

PUT A SHUNT INSIDE THE SKULL
AND TUBE IT TO THE STOMACH,
WHERE HE'LL PEE THE FLUID OUT.
MOTHER.
PEE IT OUT?
DOCTOR.
AND WITHOUT A DOUBT
WE'LL MAKE IT
SO WE CAN SEE
WHAT'S GOING ON INSIDE HIS BRAIN,
WHY SOMETHING IS AMISS
WHAT'S GOING ON INSIDE HIS BRAIN?

(DOCTOR'S pager rings.)

DOCTOR. Whoopsie. *(Reads pager.)* Cerebral hemorrhage on four. Gotta go.

(He exits.)

RHODA.
DON'T THINK OF GIVING UP.
DON'T THINK OF GIVING IN.
DON'T THINK OF ANYTHING BUT ...
MOTHER.
THE INVINCIBILITY OF ...
RHODA and MOTHER.
GORDON MICHAEL SCHWINN.

MOTHER. *(Yells)* Sweetheart!
GORDON. *(Yells)* Mother!

(They hug. She sings.)

MOTHER'S GONNA MAKE THINGS FINE

MOTHER.
MOTHER'S GONNA FILE HER NAILS.
MOTHER'S GONNA STAY SERENE.
WHAT I MEAN
IS SHE'LL PROTECT YOU.
HEY, I'M BRINGING YOU A NEW DAY.
Okay, I'm bringing you a new day.
AND EVEN THOUGH IT SHITS
MOTHER'S GONNA FIX THINGS.
TRY TO KEEP YOUR WITS.
MOTHER'S GONNA MAKE THINGS FINE.

GORDON. Ma. It's not like when I broke my arm. So drop the happy face. Okay?

IN THE DARKEST
OF DARK DESPAIR
I'LL BE FOUND
SITTING HERE
IF YOU WANT WE TO SAY LIFE'S FAIR
THAT IS SOMETHING I CAN'T SAY.

MOTHER.
ANYWAY ...
MOTHER'S GONNA DRINK CHAMPAGNE.
MA WILL HELP YOU BEAT THE ODDS.
SHE'LL EXPLAIN WHY SHE'S SO DAMN BLASÉ
BECAUSE I'M BRINGING YOU A NEW DAY.
YES, I'M WELCOMING A NEW DAY.
AND MOTHER WILL ATTEND.
MOTHER'S GONNA FIX THINGS.
MOTHER'S GONNA MEND.
MOTHER'S GONNA MAKE THINGS FINE.

GORDON.
THIS CANNOT CHANGE, MOTHER.
IT'S STRANGE, MOTHER.
BUT THIS THING'S OUTSIDE OUR CONTROL.
THIS WHOLE RIG'MAROLE
IS A JOKE I DON'T UNDERSTAND.

MOTHER.	**GORDON.**
NOTHING'S STRONGER THAN MOTHER	
	THAT'S THE WAY THINGS WERE PRE-WAR
NOTHING'S TOUGHER THAN MOTHER	THIS IS NOW AND THERE'S BEFORE
NO ONE FIGHTS AS HARD	MY WORLD HAS CHANGED
WHEN SOMETHING'S IN THE WAY	IN SUCH A WAY.
I'M BRINGING YOU A NEW DAY	SHE'S BRINGING ME A NEW DAY
GODDAMMIT, IT'S A NEW DAY	DAMMIT IT'S A NEW DAY
AND MOTHER WILL PROTECT	
MOTHER'S GONNA FIX THINGS	
ANYTHING THAT'S WRECKED.	
MOTHER'S GONNA MAKE THINGS FINE.	
OH YES, I'M BRINGING YOU A NEW DAY.	MA! SHE'S
YES, YES, YES.	BRINGING ME A NEW DAY.
A FABULOUS OLD, NEW DAY	
	A FABULOUS AND NEW DAY.

BOTH.
AND MOTHER WILL PROTECT
MOTHER'S GONNA FIX THINGS.
ANYTHING THAT'S WRECKED.
MOTHER'S GONNA MAKE THINGS —

GORDON. Mother, stop it. Haven't you heard anything I said? You can't just smile every goddamn thing away.

BE POLITE TO EVERYONE

(Where GORDON sees and responds to MR. BUNGEE, and his MOTHER thinks GORDON is talking to her.)

MR. BUNGEE. Let's try to grow up before we die, huh?
BE POLITE TO EVERYBODY.
EVERYBODY EXCEPT ALL YOUR NEAREST AND YOUR DEAREST.
THEY LOVE TOO MUCH AND EARN YOUR SPITE.
SO NEVER BE POLITE.
MOTHER. Okay, you want me to go? I'll go?
GORDON. Oh, great.
MR. BUNGEE.
BE POLITE TO THE MAILMAN.
BE POLITE TO THE BULLDOG DOWN THE STREET
BE POLITE TO THE MAN WHO SELLS SHOES
WHEN HE MEASURES YOUR FEET.
BE POLITE ALWAYS.
GORDON. You know, nobody invited you here.
MOTHER. What?
MR. BUNGEE.
TO ATHLETES IN HALLWAYS.
GORDON. Sorry, Mother — I didn't mean you.
MR. BUNGEE.
ALWAYS BE POLITE.
MOTHER. You're rude sometimes.
MR. BUNGEE.
BE POLITE.
MOTHER. You're rude to me.
MR. BUNGEE.
BE POLITE.
MOTHER. And you're rude to Roger, too.
MR. BUNGEE.
BE POLITE.
MOTHER. And by the way, honey, where is Roger?
GORDON. Where do you think?
BOTH. Sailing.

(They look at each other and shrug.)

GORDON. Goyim.

MOTHER. Roger will be here — as soon as he knows. Goodnight, Sweetheart. Get some rest.

(GORDON leans back in his bed and imagines ROGER, dressed like a sailor. ROGER enters and sings:)

I'D RATHER BE SAILING

ROGER.
I'D RATHER BE SAILING—
YES I WOULD—
ON AN OPEN SEA.
I'D STAND AT THE RAILING
IF I COULD
FEELING WILD AND FREE.
THE SUN IS ON MY NECK,
THE WIND IS IN MY FACE.
THE WATER'S INCREDIBLY BLUE,
AND . . . I'D RATHER BE SAILING,
YES, I'D WANNA GO SAIL
AND THEN COME HOME TO YOU.

SEX IS GOOD
BUT I'D RATHER BE SAILING.
FOOD IS NICE
BUT I'D RATHER BE SAILING.
PEOPLE ARE SWELL
BUT I'D RATHER BE SAILING
OVER THE HORIZON.
AND …

I'D RATHER BE SAILING
YES I WOULD

GORDON.
HE'D RATHER BE SAILING

ROGER.
ON AN OPEN SEA.

GORDON.
ON AN OPEN SEA,

ROGER.
I'D STAND THERE INHALING
IF I COULD.

GORDON.
HE'D STAND THERE INHALING

ROGER.
FEELING WILD AND FREE

GORDON.
FEELING WILD AND FREE.

ROGER.
THE SUN IS ON MY NECK
THE WIND IS IN MY FACE
THE SEA IS INCREDIBLY BLUE,

ROGER.
AND
I'D RATHER BE SAILING
YES I'D WANNA GO SAIL
AND THEN COME HOME TO YOU.
I'D RATHER BE SAILING
YES, I'D WANNA GO SAIL
AND THEN COME HOME TO YOU.

FAMILY HISTORY

NANCY D.
HELLO? HELLO! WAKE UP — HELLO!
I'M NANCY D.
THE THIN NURSE.

RICHARD. *(A large man)*
I AM THE NICE NURSE.
IF I CAN HELP YOU
PLEASE LET ME HELP YOU
'CAUSE THE OTHERS WON'T HELP YOU.
(THOSE BITCHES …)

MOTHER. Gordon, that unpleasant nurse says we have to give them a family history before the procedure.
GORDON. You do it.

(MOTHER looks at the clipboard and begins shaking her head yes and checking things off.)

MOTHER. Heart disease … obesity … mental illness … obsessive/compulsive behavior ….

ANYTHING THAT'S WRONG IS HIS FATHER'S.
ALL.
ANYTHING THAT'S WRONG IS HIS FATHER'S.

(GORDON, in his wheelchair, leads this oom-pah band of minstrels.)

GORDO'S LAW OF GENETICS

GORDON. *(Spoken.)* Uh – 1 – 2 – Uh – 1 – 2– 3– 4

RICHARD and DOCTOR.
BUM BA BUM BUM BA BUM BUM BA BUM BA BUM
BUM BA BUM BUM BA BUM

NANCY D., MINISTER, HOMELESS WOMAN, RHODA.
BAH — DOW

RICHARD and DOCTOR.
BUM BA BUM BUM BA BUM BUM BA BUM BA BUM
BUM BA BUM BUM BA BUM

LADIES.
BAH —

RICHARD and DOCTOR.	**MINISTER.**	**LADIES.**
BUM BA BUM BUM BA BUM	THE BAD TRAIT	
BUM BA BUM BA BUM	WILL ALWAYS PREDOMINATE.	
BUM BA BUM BUM BA BUM	BAD TRAIT	
BUM BA BUM BA BUM	IS CERTAIN TO WIN.	
BUM BA BUM BUM BA BUM	THE BAD TRAIT	
BUM BA BUM BA BUM	WILL ALWAYS PREDOMINATE.	
THAT IS THE LAW OF GENETICS	THAT IS THE LAW OF GENETICS ACCORDING TO	THAT IS THE LAW OF GENETICS
BUM BA BUM BUM BA BUM	SCHWINN.	
BUM BA BUM BA BUM		

RICHARD.	**MINISTER and DOCTOR.**	**LADIES.**
BUM BA BUM BUM BA BUM	BUM BA BUM BUM BA BUM	BUM BA BUM BUM BA BUM
BUM BUM BUM BUM		
		SMART OR DUMB?
	THE DUMB WILL PREDOMINATE	
BUM BA BUM BUM BA BUM		FAT OR THIN?
	THE FAT WILL PREDOMINATE	
BUM BA BUM BUM BA BUM		LAZY OR NOT LAZY?

RICHARD.	**MINISTER and DOCTOR.**	**LADIES.**
	THE LAZY WILL PREDOMINATE	
		WE HAVE
WE HAVE	WE HAVE	
LOUSY AESTHETICS	LOUSY AESTHETICS	LOUSY AESTHETICS

RICHARD and DOCTOR.	**MINISTER.**	
BUM BA BUM BUM BA BUM	THE BAD TRAIT	
BUM BA BUM BA BUM	WILL ALWAYS PREDOMINATE	WILL ALWAYS PREDOMINATE
BUM BA BUM BUM BA BUM	BAD TRAIT	
BUM BA BUM BA BUM	IS CERTAIN TO WIN.	IS CERTAIN TO WIN
BUM BA BUM BUM BA BUM	THE BAD TRAIT	THE BAD TRAIT
BUM BA BUM BA BUM	WILL ALWAYS PREDOMINATE	WILL ALWAYS PREDOMINATE
THAT IS THE LAW OF GENETICS	THAT IS THE LAW OF GENETICS	THAT IS THE LAW OF GENETICS
ACCORDING TO	ACCORDING TO	ACCORDING TO
BUM BA BUM BUM BA BUM	SCHWINN.	SCHWINN.
BUM BA BUM BA BUM		
BUM BA BUM BUM BA BUM	BUM BA BUM BUM BA BUM	BUM BA BUM BUM BA BUM
BUM BA BUM BA BUM	BUM BABUMBABUM	BUMBABUMBABUM

RHODA.
WHY IS THE SMART SON
ALWAYS THE GAY SON?

NANCY D., HOMELESS WOMAN, DOCTOR, RICHARD.
SCHWINN'S SECOND LAW OF GENETICS!

RICHARD.	**MINISTER and DOCTOR.**	**LADIES.**
BUM BA BUM BUM BA BUM		SMART OR DUMB
	THE DUMB WILL PREDOMINATE	

RICHARD.	**MINISTER and DOCTOR.**	**LADIES.**
BUM BA BUM BUM BA BUM		FAT OR THIN
	THE FAT WILL PREDOMINATE	
BUM BA BUM BUM BA BUM		LAZY OR NOT LAZY
	THE LAZY WILL PREDOMINATE	
		WE HAVE
WE HAVE	WE HAVE	
LOUSY AESTHETICS	LOUSY AESTHETICS	LOUSY AESTHETICS

RICHARD and DOCTOR.	**MINISTER.**	**RHODA.**	**HOMELESS WOMAN.**
BUM BA BUM BUM			
BA BUM	BUM BA BUM		
BUM BA BUM	BUM BA BUM	BUM BA BUM	
BA BUM	BUM BA BUM	BUM BA BUM	BUM BA BUM
BA BA BUM BUM	BA BUM	BUM BA BUM	BUM BA BUM
BA BUM	BUM BA BUM	BA BUM	BUM BA BUM
BA BUM	BUM BA BUM	BUM BA BUM	BA BUM
BA DOW!	BA DOW!	BA DOW!	BA DOW!

HOMELESS WOMAN.
SAY YOUR FATHER HAS A STOMACH—
ALL.
BUM BA BUM BUM BA BUM
HOMELESS WOMAN.
YOU ARE SURE TO GET THAT STOMACH.
RHODA and NANCY D.
IT'S A SIMPLE FACT OF SCIENCE.
MINISTER AND HOMELESS WOMAN.
DON'T RELY ON SELF-RELIANCE.
NANCY D., MINISTER, LISA, RHODA.
YOU ARE SURE TO GET THAT STOMACH SO EAT, EAT, EAT!

RICHARD and DOCTOR.	**MINISTER.**	**LADIES.**
HUMMA		
HUMMA HUMMA MUMMA	BECAUSE THE BAD	
BUM BA BUM BUM BA BUM	TRAIT	
BUM BA BUM BA BUM	WILL ALWAYS PREDOMINATE	WILL ALWAYS PREDOMINATE

RICHARD and DOCTOR.	**MINISTER.**	**LADIES.**
BUM BA BUM BUM BA BUN	BAD TRAIT	
BUM BA BUM BA BUM	IS CERTAIN TO WIN.	IS CERTAIN TO WIN
BUM BA BUM BUM	THE BAD TRAIT	THE BAD TRAIT
WILL ALWAYS PREDOMINATE.		

ALL.
THAT IS THE LAW OF GENETICS . . .
THAT IS THE LAW OF GENETICS ACCORDING TO . . .
THAT IS THE LAW OF GENETICS ACCORDING TO . . .

RICHARD and DOCTOR.
G-G-G-G-GORDO. G-G-G-G-G GORDO.

Add **MINISTER and RHODA.**
G-G-G-G-GORDO. G-G-G-G-G GORDO.

Add **HOMELESS WOMAN and NANCY D.**
G-G-G-G-GORDO. G-G-G-G-G GORDO.
G-G-G-G GORDO SCHWINN!

NANCY D., HOMELESS WOMAN, RHODA, MINISTER.	**RICHARD and DOCTOR.**
OH GORDO'S LAW OF GENETICS!	OH, YEA!

GORDON.
UH-1-2-3-4!

MINISTER and DOCTOR.		
BUM BA BUM BUM		
BA BUM		
BUM BA BUM		**NANCY D., HW, RHODA.**
BA BUM	**MINISTER.**	BA DOW!
BUM BA BUM BUM	ANYTHING THAT'S WRONG	
BA BUM	IS HIS FATHER'S.	
BUM BA BUM		
BA BUM		
BUM BA BUM BUM		
BA BUM		
		ANYTHING THAT'S WRONG IS HIS FATHER'S.

AND THEY'RE OFF

GORDON.
PONIES IN THE SUN
THE RACE IS SOON BEGINNING
MY FATHER BET THE FAMILY FORTUNE
ON A SLEEK BROWN HORSE.
MY FATHER HAD A HUNCH
WE GAVE UP LUNCH.
SO DADDY COULD MAKE A WAGER.
MOM WOULD SCOFF.

(A curtain reveals everyone but GORDON standing behind a row of walkers, like bettors at a racetrack.)

GORDON.
SHE WOULD SCOFF, HEAR HER SCOFF.
AND THEY'RE OFF!

RHODA, NANCY D., HOMELESS WOMAN, DOCTOR, MINSTER, RICHARD.
LA LA LA LA LA LA LA
LA LA LA!

YEAH, THEY'RE OFF!

LA LA LA LA LA LA LA
LA LA LA!

AND THEY MOVE IN A HERD
LIKE A FOUR-LETTER WORD
AND THEY'RE OFF

LA LA LA LA!

TICKETS FLOAT

OH—

TO THE GROUND
AND THE BAND STARTS TO PLAY

AH—

AS THE HORSES GO 'ROUND.
AND THEY'RE OFF!

AND THEY'RE OFF!

MOMMY SAT AND CRIED
BUT DAD WAS UNAFFECTED
HE SAID,
"HAVE YOU EVER HAD A BETTER TWO MINUTES
IN THE LAST THREE YEARS?"

GORDON.
WE SAID, "BUT DAD, THE DUMB HORSE LOST!"
HE SAID,
"SOMETIMES JOY HAS A TERRIBLE COST,
I KNOW THAT."
MA WOULD SCOFF, SHE WOULD
SCOFF, HEAR HER SCOFF.
AND THEY'RE OFF!

RHODA, NANCY D., HOMELESS WOMAN, DOCTOR, MINISTER, RICHARD.
LALALALALALALA
LALALA!

YEAH, THEY'RE OFF!

LALALALALALALA
LA LA LA!

MOMMY'S BITING HIS NECK
AS THEY ROLL ON THE DECK
AND THEY'RE OFF! — LA LA LA LA
THERE IS BLOOD — OH—
ON THE GROUND.
AND THE BAND STARTS TO PLAY — AH—
AS THE HORSES GO 'ROUND;
AND THEY'RE OFF! — AND THEY'RE OFF!

ISN'T LIFE FUNNY?
PEOPLE LOSE MONEY
AND HAVE FUN.
BETTING, OF COURSE, IS
HELL ON THE HORSES
AND THE FAMILIES WHERE THE BETTING IS DONE;
IT'S A JOKE TO BELIEVE SOMEONE'S WON.

ALL THEY DID WAS FIGHT.
PLUS THEY DISCUSSED THE WEATHER.
MY FATHER BET THE FAMILY FORTUNE
TILL IT DISAPPEARED.
WE ALSO LAUGHED A LOT.
THAT WAS A THING I OFTEN FORGOT
TO TELL YOU.
BUT IT'S TRUE, YES IT'S TRUE, IT IS TRUE
AND HE'S OFF!

LALALALALALALA
LA LA LA!

DADDY'S OFF.

LALALALALALALA
LA LA LA!

WE GET LETTERS FROM MAINE

WHERE HE TRIES TO EXPLAIN
WHY HE'S OFF.

LA LA LA LA!

WHAT WAS LOST — OH—
WAS NOT FOUND;
AND THE BAND STARTS TO PLAY — AH—
AS THE HORSES GO 'ROUND
AND THEY'RE O-O-O-OFF! — AND THEY'RE O-O-O-OFF!
AND THEY'RE OFF! — AND THEY'RE OFF!

(The bettors transform into horses/patients; every person behind a walker racing.)

I HEAR THE BELL OF THE STARTING GATE.

THEY ARE OFF!

WE ARE SALIVATING AS WE MOVE IT!

AND THEY MOVE IN A HERD — MOVING DOWN THE TRACK!

LIKE A FOUR-LETTER WORD
AND THEY'RE OFF!

COMING' DOWN THE STRETCH!

THERE IS BLOOD

THERE IS BLOOD

ON THE GROUND

ON THE GROUND

AND THE BAND STARTS TO PLAY — OH—
AS THE HORSES GO 'ROUND
AND 'ROUND

AND 'ROUND

AND 'ROUND

AND 'ROUND

AND 'ROUND

AND 'ROUND

AND AROUND

AND AROUND

AND 'ROUND — AND 'ROUND
AND 'ROUND — AND 'ROUND
AND AROUND — AND 'ROUND
AND 'ROUND
AND 'ROUND
AND 'ROUND
AND THEY'RE OFF! — AND THEY'RE OFF!

ROGER ARRIVES

(TABLEAU: in the room. GORDON is asleep. RHODA and MOTHER at his side. Outside the hospital: the HOMELESS WOMAN waits. ROGER passes her, looking great.)

HOMELESS WOMAN. *(As ROGER passes)*
HEY MISTER. HEY YOU.
PLEASE CAN YOU SPARE ME SOME CHANGE, SIR?
ROGER. Have a dollar.

(He reaches into his pocket and goes to hand her the bill.)

HOMELESS WOMAN.
I asked for change. Change is what I want.

(She ignores the bill and walks away; he shrugs his head and continues. He stops in the hallway. GORDON wears a big patch on his forehead.)

RHODA. *(Exuberant, but in a whisper)*
ROGER HAS ARRIVED!
MOTHER. Hallelujah!
RHODA.
ROGER HAS ARRIVED!
IN A SUIT
LOOKING FIT.
MOTHER.
ROGER'S ALWAYS DAMNED APPROPRIATE.
RHODA.
GIVE HIM YOUR FEAR,
ROGER IS HERE.

ROGER. *(Softly)*
ROGER HAS ARRIVED.
GORDON. *(Waking)*
WHAT THE FUCK TOOK YOU SO LONG?
ROGER.
NO WIND.
GORDON.
NO WIND. *(Laughing)*
ROGER. Sorry I wasn't here.
GORDON. Hey, it's not like you left *after* you found out. Did you?

ROGER. If I could do that, I'd be a lot more interesting. Rhoda, how bad is it?

RHODA. They still don't know. They have to take another picture.

MOTHER. *(Proud of her medical knowledge)* MRI.

ROGER. Mr. Claustrophobia grows up.

GORDON.
I NEED A NEW BRAIN.

RHODA and MOTHER. *(Echo)*
HE NEEDS A NEW BRAIN.

ROGER.
THAT'S NOT A CRIME.

RHODA. Listen to Roger.

GORDON.
AND I NEED A NEW BODY.

ROGER.
WELL, THAT'LL TAKE TIME.

GORDON.
I NEED A NEW BRA-A-A-A-A-A-A-AIN
WHO WILL I BE?

MOTHER. You'll still be you.

AM I INSANE?

ALL. Yes.

I NEED A NEW BRAIAIAIAIAIAIAIAIAIN
WILL I BE THE SAME OLD ME?

ROGER. You look good.

MOTHER. He looks pale.

RHODA. He looks better.

ROGER. *(To MOTHER and RHODA)*
GO GET DINNER.

MOTHER.
WE'RE NOT HUNGRY.

ROGER.
ROGER HAS ARRIVED.

(As RHODA and MOTHER kiss both of them goodbye)

MOTHER. *(To GORDON and ROGER)*
NOW WE'RE HUNGRY. *(To RHODA)*
AREN'T WE HUNGRY?

RHODA. I'm hungry.

(RHODA and MOTHER leave.)

ROGER. *(To ROGER)*
LEAN BACK.
RELAX.
RESUME ATTACKS.
AND SLEEP.

JUST GO

GORDON.
GO.
LOOK AT ME:
JUST GO.
DON'T SAY ANYTHING,
JUST GO.
I CAN'T EVEN
WALK ACROSS THE ROOM,
UNASSISTED.
SO, GO
GO AWAY —
THERE'S NOTHING LEFT TO SAY.
YOU WON'T HAVE TO WALK AND
HOLD MY
ELBOW.
HELL NO.
JUST GO.

(ROGER touches his leg.)

DON'T.
PLEASE DON'T TOUCH MY SKIN.
BECAUSE UP TO NOW I'VE BEEN
VERY STRONG.
AND SO HEROIC
YOU WOULDN'T RECOGNIZE ME.
GO — GO — GOODBYE.
CAUSE IF YOU MAKE ME CRY
THEN I'LL PROB'LY HAVE TO KILL YOU.
I WILL, YOU
KNOW. JUST GO.
ROGER.
SOMETIMES YOU'RE A DOOZY.
JESUS WHEN YOU TALK
I FEEL SO DAMN WOOZY
YOU'RE SO CRAZY.

(ROGER gets into bed next to GORDON.)

GORDON. Only a little crazy.

ROGER.
GO AHEAD AND USE ME.
MAKE A PASS
AND I
WILL SAVE YOUR —
ASS.

GO. *(Grabbing ROGER's arm to his chest)*
LOOK AT ME:
JUST GO.

I'M NOT GOING NOWHERE.

DON'T SAY ANYTHING,
JUST GO.

THAT'S A ROW WE'LL HOE,
DEAR.

I CAN'T EVEN
WALK ACROSS THE ROOM,

LATER ON

UNASSISTED.
SO, GO
GO, GOODBYE —
CAUSE IF YOU MAKE ME CRY

LATER ON —

THEN I'LL PROB'LY HAVE TO
KILL YOU

AND I'LL PROB'LY HAVE
TO KILL YOU

I WILL, YOU
KNOW,

GORDON.
JUST GO.

ROGER.
NO.

GORDON.
NO.

ROGER.
SCHMO.

OPERATION TOMORROW

(RICHARD, the nice nurse, comes barging in.)

RICHARD. Visiting hours are over, boys.
TIME TO GO TO SLEEP.
GORDO NEEDS HIS REST.
TIME TO GO TO SLEEP.
HE'LL BE BRAVE AS ZORRO.
MUST BE AT HIS BEST:
MRI IS TOMORROW.

GORDON. How delightful.

POOR, UNSUCCESSFUL AND FAT

(MUSIC for "POOR, UNSUCCESSFUL, AND FAT" begins. MINISTER enters.)

MINISTER.
SCHWINN: IS THAT GERMAN PROTESTANT?
GORDON.
SCHWINN IS GERMAN JEWISH.
MINISTER.
OH WELL, THE LORD IS KIND AND ALL-KNOWING.
GORDON.
THANK YOU FOR COMING.
THANK YOU FOR GOING.

(The MINISTER leaves.)

RICHARD. Time for your sponge bath.
GORDON. Must I?
RICHARD. Honey, I don't want to be here, either. *(Washes GORDON as he sings)*
POOR, UNSUCCESSFUL AND FAT.
WHO WOULD'VE THOUGHT I WOULD END LIKE THAT?
SURELY IN NO TIME
YOU'LL BE BACK TO NORMAL
IN YOUR EVENING FORMAL.
I'LL BE POOR, UNSUCCESSFUL
POOR, UNSUCCESSFUL AND FAT.
AND GETTING OLDER.

PLUS, HAVE YOU NOTICED I SWEAT?
I HAVE A LIST OF THINGS I REGRET.
DON'T ELL THIS STORY TO LITTLE CHILDREN,
'CAUSE IT'S GONNA SCARE THEM,
HOW I'M POOR, UNSUCCESSFUL
POOR, UNSUCCESSFUL ND FAT.
AND GETTING OLDER.
GETTING GRAYER.
STOP ME IF YOU'VE HEARD THIS BEFORE,
'CAUSE IF YOU'VE HEARD THIS BEFORE
HELL, IT'S JUST MORE OF THE SAME.
GORDON.
WELL . . .

RICHARD.
HELP ME, I'M A PLAYER.
WHO'LL NEVER MAKE IT.
I WON'T MAKE IT.
I WON'T MAKE IT.

GORDON.
NO NO NO NO NO NO NO NO

RICHARD.
ONCE I WAS PRACTIC'LY THIN.
NOW I CAN EAT LIKE I'M RIN TIN TIN.
SOON YOU'LL BE BACK HOME — A SUCCESS IN TRAINING,
I'LL BE HERE COMPLAINING
THAT I'M POOR, UNSUCCESSFUL,
POOR, UNSUCCESSFUL AND FAT.
AND GETTING OLDER.

I'M GETTING OLDER.

GORDON.
I AM NOT SUCCESSFUL
I AM NOT SO DAMN SUCCESSFUL

I AM NOT SUCCESSFUL
I AM NOT SO DAMN SUCCESSFUL

(BUNGEE appears in the rear window.)

RICHARD.
I'M GETTING OLDER.

I'M GETTING OLDER.

BUNGEE.
YOU ARE NOT SUCCESSFUL.

GORDON.
I AM NOT SUCCESSFUL.

BUNGEE.
YOU'RE TOO OLD TO BE A FAILURE.

GORDON.
I'M TOO OLD TO BE A FAILURE

BUNGEE.
YOUR FUTURE'S LOOKING CLOUDY

GORDON.
MY FUTURE'S LOOKING CLOUDY

BUNGEE.
YOUR SISTER IS A WHORE.

GORDON. My sister is a receptionist.

BUNGEE.
BET YOUR TUSH YOU'RE UNSUCCESSFUL.
DON'T MEAN TO MAKE THIS MORE STRESSFUL
THAT IT'S ALREADY BECOME.
BUT YOU'RE POOR, UNSUCCESSFUL AND DUMB.
POOR, UNSUCCESSFUL AND DUMB AND UNTALENTED.
GORDON. Ugh.
BUNGEE.
POOR, UNSUCCESSFUL AND DUMB
AND UNTALENTED.
POOR, UNSUCCESSFUL AND DUMB
AND UNTALENTED.
POOR, UNSUCCESSFUL AND DUMB
AND UNTALENTED.

GORDON.
SHUT UP!

SITTING BECALMED IN THE LEE OF CUTTYHUNK

(An MRI is wheeled in. Everyone but NANCY D. helps GORDON onto the sliding piece, then slide him into the MRI.)

NANCY D.
HELLO! HOORAY!
GET UP! HOORAY!
TODAY IS NOT A GOOD DAY.
BECAUSE TODAY IS MRI DAY.
MRI DAY'S THE DAY YOU FEEL THEY BURY YOU ALIVE.
I JIVE.

THE SHAPE, THE FEEL.
AN AIRTIGHT SEAL.
TODAY IS NOT A GOOD DAY.

GORDON. Help!
NANCY D. Now relax and try not to move.
RICHARD. It only takes forty-five minutes.
DOCTOR. You might not want to open your eyes.
MOTHER. Think calm thoughts.
ROGER. Think sailing.
GORDON. Sailing.

ROGER, GORDON, DOCTOR, MINISTER, HOMELESS WOMAN, RICHARD, MOTHER, RHODA, NANCY D.
SITTING BECALMED

IN THE LEE OF CUTTYHUNK
WAITING FOR THE WIND TO BLOW.
WAILING FOR THE WIND TO CARRY US
SOMEWHERE, SOMEHOW.
SITTING BECALMED.

(A camera in the MRI begins capturing GORDON's face. The image is displayed in the rear WINDOW.)

ALL.
IN THE LEE, IN THE LEE, IN THE LEE
IN THE LEE, IN THE LEE, IN THE LEE,
IN THE LEE OF CUTTYHUNK.
HEY! HEY! HEY! HEY! HEY!

GORDON.
THIS IS YOUR IDEA OF A VACATION.
WHAT A GOOD IDEA FOR RECREATION.
AT LEAST IT'S SUNNY IN NEWPORT.
AT LEAST IT'S
SUNNY ON CAPE COD
AT LEAST IT'S
SUNNY IN NANTUCKET.
OH, YEAH, FUCK IT.
I HATE THE SUN.

ALL.
AT LEAST IT'S

AT LEAST IT'S

ALL.
BUT WE ARE SITTING BECALMED
IN THE LEE OF CUTTYHUNK.
HOTTER THAN A PREGNANT COW.
WAITING FOR THE WIND TO CARRY US
SOMEWHERE, SOMEHOW.
SITTING BECALMED
IN THE LEE, IN THE LEE, IN THE LEE,
IN THE LEE, IN THE LEE, IN THE LEE,
IN THE LEE OF

GORDON and RHODA.
CUTTYHUNK.

WHEW!

HEY! HEY!
HEY! HEY!
HEY!

ALL OTHERS.
CUTTYHUNK.
CUTTYHUNK.

WHEW!

HEY! HEY!
HEY! HEY!
HEY!

GORDON.
LIFE IS SHORT
SAILING IS LOOOOOOOOOONG.
ANYONE GOT A NEWSPAPER?
ALL.
SITTING IN THE LEE OF CUTTYHUNK.
GORDON.
ANYONE GOT A CROSSWORD PUZZLE?
ALL.
SITTING IN THE LEE OF CUTTYHUNK.
GORDON.
ANYONE GOT AN ANYTHING?
ALL BUT ROGER.
SITTING IN THE LEE, IN THE LEE, IN THE LEE IN THE —

ROGER.
WOULD IT KILL YOU TO TRY
TO ENJOY THIS A LITTLE BIT?
THIS IS MY FAVORITE THING IN THE WORLD.
WHY ARE YOU SUCH AN ASS?
GORDON.
CAPTAIN, CAN WE USE GAS?
ALL.
NO! NO. NO. . . .
GORDON. *(To ROGER)*
WHEN YOU'RE RIGHT, YOU'RE RIGHT.

ALL BUT GORDON.	**GORDON.**
COULDN'T YOU TRY	
TO ENJOY THIS A LITTLE BIT?	AND YOU'RE RIGHT.
THIS IS OUR FAVORITE	I'M SUCH A JERK-OFF.
THING IN THE WORLD!	
	Right.

ROGER.
WAIT, I HEAR IT.
RHODA.
WAIT, IT'S COMING.
ALL.
WAIT. I FEEL THE WIND.

WHOOSH. . . .

WHOOSH. . . .

I THINK WE'RE MOVING!
I THINK WE'RE MOVING!
NOT BECALMED!

GORDON.
COULD THAT BE A METAPHOR?
ALL.
CUTTYHUNK IS IN OUR PAST.
GORDON.
GETTING SOMEWHERE AT LAST
IS A SIGN OF THINGS IMPROVING.
ALL.
NOT BECALMED!
IN THE LEE, IN THE LEE, IN THE LEE
IN THE LEE, IN THE LEE, IN THE LEE,
IN THE LEE OF
RHODA, RICHARD, DOCTOR, NANCY D.
CUTTYHUNK.

NANCY D. We got the picture.
RICHARD. That wasn't so bad, was it?

RHODA, RICHARD, DOCTOR, NANCY D.	**ROGER, MOTHER, HOMELESS WOMAN, MINISTER.**
	HEY! HEY! HEY! HEY!
IN THE LEE OF	
CUT CUT CUTTYHUNK.	HEY!

GORDON, NANCY RICHARD.	**MOTHER, ROGER.**	**MINISTER, HOMELESS WOMAN.**
CUTTYHUNK CUTTYHUNK	CUTTYHUNK.	CUTTYHUNK.
CUTTYHUNK CUTTYHUNK	HEY HEY	
CUTTYHUNK CUTTYHUNK	HEY HEY	
CUTTYHUNK CUTTYHUNK	HEY	
CUTTYHUNK CUTTYHUNK		
CUTTYHUNK CUTTYHUNK	HEY HEY	
CUTTYHUNK CUTTYHUNK	HEY HEY	
CUTTYHUNK CUTTYHUNK	HEY	HEY HEY
CUTTYHUNK CUTTYHUNK		HEY HEY
CUTTYHUNK CUTTYHUNK		

ALL.
HEY HEY HEY HEY
HEY!

(The MRI procedure is finished. The DOCTOR and others gather

around the image.)

CRANIOTOMY

(GORDON is in a wheelchair. The DOCTOR is checking x-rays, then sings.)

DOCTOR. *(Looking at the MRI)*
SON OF A GUN, I SEE IT.
YOUR BLOOD VESSEL'S PINCHED AND COI-LED.
GORDO, NOW I HAVE
A NAME FOR WHAT YOU HAVE;
AND YOUR DESIGNATION.
Add **NANCY D.**
ARTERIAL VENOUS MALFORMATION.
GORDON. And that is?
NANCY D. Arterial venous malformation. Just something you were born with.
VEINS IN THE BRAINS ARE LIKE BALLOONS
FILLED WITH WATER.
SOMETIMES THEY BURST.
IF WORSE COMES TO WORST,
WHICH UNFORTUNATELY YOURS DID.
DOCTOR.
CRANIOTOMY
IS INDICATED.
CRANIOTOMY
THAT IS WHAT YOU NEED.
YOU MUST RELY ON ME,
I'M VERY HIGHLY RATED.
AD CRANIOTOMY
IS HOW I'D PROCEED.
RIGHT?
NANCY D.
RIGHT.
DOCTOR.
RIGHT?
GORDON.
WELL —
NANCY D. We should tell him.
DOCTOR.
IF I'M NOT EXACT
I MAY CRUSH THE MOTOR TRACT

NANCY D.
SO THE BAD NEWS IS:
YOU MAY NEVER RUN OR HIKE
OR RIDE A BIKE.
EVEN WORSE NEWS IS:
YOU MAY SIMPLY DIE.

DOCTOR. Of course, it's entirely your decision.

MINISTER.
IT'S A HIGH-RISK OPERATION.
HE CAN'T GUARANTEE SUCCESS.

DOCTOR. I wish I could.

MINISTER,
BUT YOU REALLY HAVE NO OPTIONS
SO THE ONLY ANSWER, MORE OR LESS.
IS ABSOLUTELY YES.
HE CAN'T GUARANTEE SUCCESS.

DOCTOR. No one can.

MINISTER.
BUT YOU REALLY HAVE NO OPTIONS
SO THE ONLY ANSWER, MORE OR LESS,
IS ABSOLUTELY YES.
ABSOLUTELY YES.

DOCTOR.
AND NOW I HAVE TO GO.
MY KIDS AND I
HAVE TICKETS TO CHICAGO.
WELL? *(Waits for GORDON to sign. GORDON signs.)*
GOOD.

DOCTOR, NANCY D., MINISTER. *(Exiting)*
SO CRANIOTOMY TOMORROW.

INVITATION TO SLEEP IN MY ARMS

RHODA. Now that we know what the problem is. We're gonna get it fixed. At least we know it's not cancer. Anyway, you'll be home in no time.

GORDON.
TOMORROW,
THEY'LL STRAP ME DOWN ON A BED
AND REMOVE THE TOP OF MY HEAD,
WHICH IS WHY I DON'T THINK
THAT NOW'S THE RIGHT TIME

GORDON.
TO HAVE TOO MUCH HOPE.
I MAY BE A DOPE,
BUT I DON'T THINK SO,
I DON'T THINK SO.
NO, I DON'T THINK SO.

ROGER.
WOULD YOU EVER
CONSIDER
LYING CLOSE TO ME TONIGHT?
FORGET YOUR WRITING.
I'M INVITING YOU TO SLEEP IN MY ARMS.
MAYBE WE'LL LAUGH TOO LOUD
MAYBE WE'LL DANCE AND YOU WILL SING.
MAYBE WE'LL SMILE AT ALL THE PLEASURES
SEX AND EATING OFTEN BRING.
MAYBE WE'LL SAY NO WORDS.
JUST SAYING NOTHING IS SUBLIME.
MAYBE WE'LL READ A BOOK YOU ALWAYS MEANT TO
READ
FOR WHICH YOU HADN'T FOUND THE TIME.

(RHODA's cell phone rings.)

RHODA. Hello? *(She hm-hm's a little.)*
EXCUSE ME,
BUT BUNGEE'S CALLING TO STATE
HOW, THOUGH HE KNOWS YOU'RE ABOUT TO SEDATE,
BUT TOMORROW AT TEN,
HE NEEDS THE "YES SONG."
GORDON. Fuck him.
RHODA.
HE SAID NO MATTER WHAT,
HE'S GOING TO REHEARSE THE "YES SONG."
GORDON. He'll wait.
RHODA.
HE SAID HIS SON, "MR. MUSIC,"
WROTE A VERSE OF THE "YES SONG"
HE'S GOING TO USE
IF YOUR SONG ISN'T FINISHED.

TONIGHT, THEN,
JUST DISREGARD WHAT HE SAID,

AND SIT AND REMINISCE WITH ROGER INSTEAD.
IF YOU GET OVERANXIOUS, PICK UP A PEN
FINISH THE SONG.
MAYBE I'M WRONG.
BUT I DON'T THINK SO.
NO, I DON'T THINK SO.
NO, I DON'T THINK SO.

	GORDON.
	I'D LOVE TO LOVE,
	BUT NEED TO WRITE.
	I GET DISTRACTED
ROGER.	SO DAMN EASILY.
FORGET THE WRITING,	
I'M INVITING YOU	THERE ARE OTHER NIGHTS
	I'LL HAVE
TO SLEEP IN MY ARMS.	TO SLEEP IN YOUR ARMS.
AND IF YOU SNORE,	I SHOULD'VE DONE
	WHAT I MEANT TO DO.
I'LL LET YOU SNORE.	I COULD'VE BEEN
	WHAT I MEANT TO BE.
MAYBE THERE'S MORE	I COULD'VE WRITTEN
	THE SCORE TO OUR LIVES —
MAYBE THERE'S MORE.	OR A SYMPHONY.
	A SIMPLE SYMPHONY.

ROGER.	**GORDON.**	**RHODA.**
MAYBE WE'LL SAY NO WORDS	A SIMPLE SYMPHONY,	I'M JUST AFRAID
		THAT YOU'LL LOSE THIS JOB
JUST SAYING NOTHING	A SIMPLE SYMPHONY,	'CAUSE BUNGEE'S BUNGEE
IS SUBLIME		YOU'LL LOSE THIS JOB
MAYBE WE'LL READ A BOOK	A SIMPLE SYMPHONY	
YOU ALWAYS MEANT TO READ.		YOU NEED THIS JOB.

GORDON. Look, it's my decision, okay.

MOTHER.
NOBODY ASKED MY OPINION, BUT:
WHY DON'T YOU TELL HIM
HIS WAS THE BEST INVITATION? *(To others)*
WHY IS HE MAKING SUCH A SCENE. *(To GORDON)*

MOTHER.
WHILE YOU SIT DISCUSSING WHAT YOU'VE GOTTA DISCUSS,
I'M OFF TO *YOUR* PLACE FOR A DATE
WITH MR. CLEAN,
I LOVE HIM.

LIE WITH THE MAN!
WHADDAYA, STUPID?
GO AND FLY WITH THE MAN —
AT LEAST TONIGHT GO FLY,
WHILE I
DEPART IN HOPE
AND NOT IN SORROW. *(Kissing all of them goodbye)*
GOODBYE, MY LOVES, GOODBYE.
OPERATION TOMORROW.

(She exits with RHODA. GORDON sings to ROGER.)

GORDON.
TONIGHT, THOUGH
MAY BE MY VERY LAST CHANCE
TO WRITE A SOMETHING I COULD BE REMEMBERED BY . . . .
IT MAY NOT BE A GREAT SONG.
BUT IT COULD BE MY LAST SONG
AND I HOPE YOU'LL UNDERSTAND
IF I SIMPLY KISS YOUR HAND.
AND SAY GOODNIGHT.

(ROGER slowly kises GORDON goodnight, then leaves.)

CHANGE

(The HOMELESS WOMAN enters in the audience. The MUSIC begins and she's asking for change.)

HOMELESS WOMAN.
Hey, can you spare some change?
How about you? Spare some change?
Can you spare some change?
Thanks, big spender.

PENNIES OR NICKELS OR DIMES.
WE LIVE IN PERILOUS TIMES.

I DON'T ASK YOU TO TREAT ME NICE.
I'M NOT ASKING FOR PLEASANT CONVERSATION.
I'M NOT ASKING FOR PARADISE.
ALL I'M ASKING FOR IS CHANGE.

HATE ME BUT DON'T KICK MY SHINS.
I'M WHERE YOUR KINDNESS BEGINS.
PLEASE, FOLKS, DO NO SPEND TIME WITH ME.
I WON'T ASK YOU TO TREAT ME LIKE YOUR MOTHER.
I'M NOT ASKING FOR SYMPATHY.
ALL I'M ASKING FOR IS CHANGE.

CHANGE THE GOVERNMENT,
KILL THE MAYOR.
IT'S NOT FA-IR HOW LIVES EVAPORATE.
CHANGE THE SYSTEM
THAT MADE US WHAT WE ARE.
I DON'T ASK FOR HUGS.
JUST NEED MONEY TO BUY MORE DRUGS.
AND IF YOU FOLKS PAY,
I'LL GO AWAY.

PEOPLE WALK BY ME WITH GLEE.
I AM WHAT THEY'LL NEVER BE.
I DON'T ASK YOU TO TIP YOUR HAT.
I DON'T ASK THAT YOU NOTICE WHAT I'M WEARING.
I COULD CARE LESS FOR THINGS LIKE THAT.
ALL I'M ASKING FOR IS CHANGE.
CHANGE.
CHANGE.
CHANGE.

PENNIES OR NICKELS OR DIMES.
WE LIVE IN PERILOUS TIMES.

YES

(RICHARD wheels GORDON onto stage. GORDON is playing a little electric piano, auditioning his song for RICHARD.)

GORDON. And so, boys and girls, before I hop back to my lily pad, I leave you with one last thought:
YES IS A GOOD WORD.

RICHARD. *(Trying to be supportive)* Go on.
GORDON.
NO IS A BAD WORD.
RICHARD. You're tellin' me.
GORDON.
THE PREFERRED WORD
IN ANY KIND OF SITUATION IS
YES, I CAN.
OH, YES, I'D LIKE TO DO THAT.
YES, THE WORLD'S INCREASINGLY ABSURD.
YES YES YES
IS A GOOD WORD
YES YES YES
IS A VERY SPECIAL WORD.

(To RICHARD.) IT WILL BE SUNG,
I GUARANTEE IT.
YOU'RE GONNA SEE IT
ON TV. IT
WILL BE SUNG.

(On the other side of the stage, BUNGEE is walking in followed by the DOCTOR with a director's chair, nurse NANCY D. as script girl and the MINISTER photographing the whole thing.)

GORDON.
YES IS A GOOD WORD.

NO IS A BAD WORD.

THE PREFERRED WORD
IN ANY KIND OF SITUATION ...

BUNGEE. *(Delightedly reading the pages.)*
YES IS A GOOD WORD.

NO IS A BAD WORD.

(The director's chair unintentionally hits BUNGEE. He explodes.)

BUNGEE. Don't touch me.
YES I WILL DO THAT
YES I WILL GO THERE
YES I WILL LIVE A GOOD AND TRUE LIFE
YES I'LL SURVIVE WHATEVER YOU THROW AT ME.
YES THE WORLD IS GRAND.
WHEN THERE'S A MOMENT,
GRAB IT AND SHAKE IT
TAKE IT

IN YOUR HAND.
YES I WILL
YES I CAN
YES I MIGHT
YES I WILL PUT UP AND HONEST FIGHT.

(BUNGEE seems very happy with the song. In the next verse, the health care professionals all start to sing back-up, like The Supremes, joined by GORDON.)

GORDON, NANCY D., MINISTER, DOCTOR.	**BUNGEE.**
YES I'LL BE FEARLESS	
	YES I'LL BE FEARLESS
YES I'LL BE HONEST	
	YES I'LL BE HONEST
YES I WILL LIVE MY LIFE WITH EMOTION	
	LIVE WITH EMOTION
YES I HAVE COURAGE	
YES AND DEVOTION	
YES I WILL SURVIVE	YES I WILL SURVIVE
BUNGEE.	**GORDON, NANCY D. MINISTER, DOCTOR.**
YES IS THE WORD THAT	AH.
OPENS THE DOOR TOO	AH.
BEING MOST ALIVE.	AH.
YES THERE'S JOY	YES.
YES THERE'S LOVE	YES.
YES THERE'S SING	YES.
YES I ABSOLUTELY HAVE TO SING.	YES.
YES YES YES	YES YES YES.
IS A GOOD WORD	YES YES YES
BUNGEE.	**GORDON, NANCY D., MINISTER, DOCTOR.**
YES YES YES	YES YES YES
IS A VERY SPECIAL WORD.	IS A VERY SPECIAL WORD.
EXCEPT WHEN A STRANGER SAYS	
GET INTO MY CAR,	**EVERYBODY.**
SAY NO.	NO!

BUNGEE. *(Getting angrier)*
OR WHEN SOMEONE SAYS
WOULD YOU LIKE TO LOSE
YOUR VIRGINITY?
SOMEONE WITH WHOM
YOU HAVE NO AFFINITY.
SAY NO NO NO NO!

EVERYBODY.
NO NO NO NO!

(Shouting)
NO NO NO NO!

CHORUS. *(Underneath)*
YES IS A GOOD WORD.
NO IS A BAD WORD.
THE PREFERRED WORD
IN ANY KIND OF SITUATION
WOULD BE: *(Fade out.)*

BUNGEE.
What is this nonsense about virginity?
This is a goddamn children's show.
I never know what you're writing about, Schwinn.
I want a song: Yes, I will do my homework.
Yes, I will work in the garden.
Yes, I will go with my grandparents … to Israel.
Instead I get this nonsense about someone
Who loses their virginity to *(disbelievingly)* those with
Whom they have no "affinity."
A-ffin-i-ty? This is a
Goddamn children's show.
Look, you're sick, you're in the hospital,
You got this brain thing.
But you know what: I'm gonna get my son to write the song.
Where's my son?
Where's my son?
Where's my son?

IN THE MIDDLE OF THE ROOM

(GORDON is alone onstage in his wheelchair.)

GORDON.
HERE I SIT
IN THE MIDDLE OF THE ROOM.
I DON'T THROW A FIT
AND I DON'T START CRYING.

NURSES FLIT
AS THEY FIDDLE IN THE ROOM.
IT'S A DAMN CHARADE
THAT I CAN'T ABIDE.

FROGGY CAME.
FROGGY WENT.
I RESENT
HIS APPEARANCE.

SPLICING VEINS.
TRICKY SHIT.
THAT IS WHAT HE SAID.
FACT REMAINS:
I COULD SOON BE DEAD.

IN THE MIDDLE OF MY GLOOM,
IN THE MIDDLE OF MY FRIGHT.
IN THE MIDDLE OF MY ROOM,
IN THE MIDDLE OF THE NIGHT.

(On the other side of the stage, his MOTHER sings.)

<table>
<tr><td></td><td>MOTHER.
HERE IS STAND IN THE MIDDLE OF THE ROAD</td></tr>
<tr><td>IN THE MIDDLE OF THE ROOM</td><td></td></tr>
<tr><td></td><td>AND I'M WAITING FOR A CAR</td></tr>
<tr><td>AND I'M WAITING FOR A SHOT</td><td></td></tr>
<tr><td></td><td>TO COME ALONG AND KILL ME.</td></tr>
<tr><td>(Yells.) Nurse please!</td><td></td></tr>
<tr><td></td><td>PEOPLE ASK WHY I'M STANDING IN THE ROAD</td></tr>
<tr><td>I AM SITTING IN THE ROOM</td><td></td></tr>
<tr><td></td><td>AND I SAY, "BECAUSE . . .</td></tr>
<tr><td>I'M AFRAID WITH WHAT I GOT</td><td></td></tr>
<tr><td></td><td>I AM FRIGHTENED HE WILL</td></tr>
<tr><td>I'LL DIE.</td><td>DIE."</td></tr>
<tr><td>KILL ME PLEASE
STRAIGHT AHEAD
MAKE ME DEAD
GET IT OVER
WITH.</td><td>KILL ME PLEASE
STRAIGHT AHEAD
MAKE ME DEAD
GET IT OVER
WITH.</td></tr>
</table>

(MOTHER calls GORDON from her cellular phone. The phone rings in his hospital room. He picks it up.)

MOTHER. I just called to tell you everything is going to be alright.
GORDON. Ma, you sound foolish.

MOTHER.
MOTHER WILL PROTECT.
MOTHER'S GONNA FIX THINGS:
ANYTHING THAT'S WRECKED
MOTHER'S GONNA MAKE THEM FINE.

GORDON.
MOTHER PLEASE,
SAY GOODBYE,
MA, A HEART TO HEART.
WHEN I DIE,
YOU CAN'T FALL APART.

MOTHER.
WHAT A STUPID THING TO SAY!
RATHER STAB ME WITH A KNIFE!
WHAT AN IGNORANT DISPLAY
IN THE MIDDLE OF YOUR LIFE!
THE MIDDLE OF YOUR . . .
IN THE MIDDLE OF YOUR . . .

GORDON. It's not in the middle of my life, mother. I'm dying.
MOTHER. I will see you tomorrow.

(She disconnects. RICHARD enters.)

RICHARD.
I AM THE NICE NURSE.
IF I CAN HELP YOU
PLEASE LET ME HELP YOU.

GORDON.
RICHARD . . .

THROW IT OUT

(MOTHER at GORDON's studio. Coke cans are everywhere, books

are piled high. She's putting books in boxes.)

MOTHER.
CLEAN AND POLISH.
MOP AND GLO
HIS STUDIO
TILL ALL IS GLEAMING.
FIRMLY, I'LL DEMOLISH
ANY SORT OF MAYHEM IN THIS PLACE.
AH – AH
O GOD
WHAT A MESS.
BOOKS SCATTERED ALL OVER.
I DON'T WANT TO GUESS
HOW LONG HE'LL LIVE
OR IF HE'LL LIVE.

HE BETTER LIVE.

STUPID BOOKS.
ALL HIS READING . . .
HIS BRAIN'S BLEEDING —
I KNOW WHY.
'CAUSE OF BOOKS.
THE HAVE MADE HIS BRAIN EXPLODE.

DAMN THESE BOOKS.
SO MUCH FLOTSAM.
I COULD PLOTZ, AM
I DISTRESSED? (YOU BETCHA)
WHO'D HAVE GUESSED
BOOKS WOULD MAKE HIS BRAIN EXPLODE?

BOOK CALLED "MOTHER COURAGE"
ALWAYS ABOUT MOTHERS.
WHAT ABOUT THE OTHERS?
FATHERS AND THE BROTHERS?
THROW IT OUT.

HERE'S "A MOTHER'S KISSES."
ALWAYS IT'S THE MISSUS.
NEVER IT'S THE *TATEH*.
LITERARY *SCHMATA*.
THROW IT OUT.

MOTHER.
IF I DON'T THROW OUT THE BOOKS,
I WILL THROW MYSELF OUT THE WINDOW.

ASSHOLE.
YESSIR, HE'S AN ASSHOLE.
HOW CAN BE JUST SIT THERE
THINKING HE WILL DIE.

ASSHOLE.
WHERE'S HIS FIGHT AND VIGOR?
THIS THEN IS MY RIGOR-
OUS REPLY.

BOOK BY NORMAN MAILER.
TOUGH GUY.
THROW IT OUT.
EGOTISTIC JEW.
"HOW TO MEET A SAILOR."
GOOD SON.
THROW IT OUT.
WHAT'S A MOM TO DO?

"SEARCH FOR WARREN HARDING."
WHO'S HE?
SHOW HIM OUT.
I JUST KEEP DISCARDING.
YOU'LL SEE —
THROW IT OUT.
AND YOU'LL COME THROUGH.
WHERE'S WHAT YOU DO.
THROW IT OUT.

I TRUST
HE WON'T SEE ME CRYING.
I'LL KEEP ON DENYING
WHAT'S BECOMING CLEAR.
IT'S JUST —
EVEN THOUGH HE'S DYING
HE WILL SEE ME LAUGH AND JOKE AND SNEER.

THROWING OUT IS PETTY
WHICH I MUST ADMIT,
BUT IT'S DEEPLY FELT.

STILL I'M GETTING READY.
TO DEAL WITH THE SHIT
I'VE BEEN LATELY DEALT.

BYE BYE GOES HIS TROLLOPE!
BYE-BYE!
LIFE SURE PACKS A WALLOP
WHICH I WON'T DENY!
BUT WE'LL COME THROUGH.
HERE'S WHAT WE'LL DO:
THROW IT OUT.

LONG LIVE WHAT'S MINE.
SCREW ALL OF GERTRUDE STEIN.
THROW.
THROW.
THROW.
THROW.
THROW IT OUT!

IN THE MIDDLE OF THE ROOM, PART 2

(GORDON is lying on his hospital bed.)

GORDON.
HERE I LIE
IN THE MIDDLE OF THE NIGHT,
AND I HAVE TO TRY
TO NOT THINK I'M DYING.

NURSES SIGH
AS THEY WELCOME IN THE LIGHT.
AND I ASK THEM WHY
THEY'RE NOT BEING MEAN.

SIX-FIFTEEN,
QUARTER OF;
I SEND LOVE
EVERY WHICH WAY.

EIGHT O'CLOCK,
HALF PAST NINE,
SURGERY'S DELAYED.

GORDON.
I RECLINE.
NOT A BIT DISMAYED.

IN THE MIDDLE OF MY BRAIN,
IN THE MIDDLE OF THE SKY,
I WOULD LIKE TO ENTERTAIN,
BUT I'LL MERELY SAY GOODBYE.

(During the MUSIC ORDERLIES transfer GORDON from the bed to a gurney and wheel him from the room.)

A REALLY LOUSY DAY IN THE UNIVERSE

(In the rear WINDOW, buildings change to street level. The HOMELESS WOMAN starts on the stairs in the theatre and speaks to ROGER onstage. She quickly moves onstage.)

HOMELESS WOMAN.
HEY! MISTER.
HEY YOU!
WHAT ARE YOU LOOKIN' SO SAD FOR?

ROGER.
NOTHING, REALLY NOTHING.
ABSOLUTELY NOTHING.
HOW ABOUT SOME MONEY?

HOMELESS WOMAN.
I CAN'T REFUSE
I NEED NEW SHOES.
AND SOME PANTS.
I NEED ROMANCE.
WHAT ABOUT YOU?

ROGER.
TONIGHT
AFTER EIGHT LONG HOURS
HE APPEARED.
IT WAS WORSE THAN THE DOCTORS HAD FEARED.
AND THEN THE DOCTOR SAID:

I HOPED BY NOW HE'D BE AWAKE
AT LEAST I THOUGHT HE'D BE AWAKE . . .

MY MISTAKE.
THEN I PRODDED HIM AND POKED HIM.
AND HIS MOTHER STARTED CRYING.
AND THEN RHODA STARTED YELLING AT THE NURSE.
IT WAS A REALLY LOUSY DAY IN THE UNIVERSE.

HOMELESS WOMAN.
YOU LOVE HIM.
TOO BAD.
WHAT ARE YOU LOOKING SURPRISED FOR.

ROGER.
WE HOPED THINGS WOULD TURN OUT BETTER.

HOMELESS WOMAN.
THINGS DON'T GET BETTER.
THEY ONLY SEEM TO.
THEN THEY DON'T.
DON'T BE SURPRISED
WHEN LIFE TURNS OUT TO BE
A TRASHY OLD CATASTROPHE AND . . . *(She sees him sobbing.)*
HEY, MISTER. *(She kind of hugs him.)*
IT'S ALL RIGHT.
LIFE IS A ROTTEN OCCASION.

ROGER.
LET ME GIVE YOU SOME MONEY.

HOMELESS WOMAN,
PLEASE FORGET THE MONEY.
PLEASE DO NOT INSULT ME.
I'M NOT AMUSED.

ROGER.
BUT IT'S THERAPY.

HOMELESS WOMAN.
I GIVE THERAPY FOR FREE.
I'M JUST GLAD TO HAVE A CLIENT FINALLY.

ROGER.
SO I CALLED HIS NAME AND HUGGED HIM
BUT THE JERK IS IN A COMA,
AND HIS MOTHER HOPES HE DIES IF HE GETS WORSE.
IT WAS A REALLY LOUSY DAY IN THE UNIVERSE.

HOMELESS WOMAN.
THEY ALL ARE.
THEY ALL ARE.

(They leave the stage with her arm draped around his back.)

BRAIN DEAD

(The beginning of the coma dream sequence; in the rear WINDOW is a mockup of GORDON lying in bed with his hair wrapped in bandages. He appears on the stage with his hair wrapped as in the mockup.)

GORDON.
BRAIN DEAD.
THAT'S WHAT I AM, LYING HERE.
I'M BRAIN DEAD.
WHAT A MESS I GOT US INTO.
BRAIN DEAD.
EVERYBODY'S SETTING OF ALARMS.

BABY, MAYBE, LIFT MY HEAD.

I SEE
I JUST PULLED A DOOZIE.
DON'T ASK: WHY ME?
ROGER, PASS THE UZI.
AS THE M.D.
LIFTS ME IN HIS CRUISY
CHISELED ARMS.

BRAIN DEAD.
STUPID AND THOUGHTLESS
IS WHAT I AM.
'CAUSE I'M BRAIN DEAD
AND GOD DAMN.

(ROGER enters and they dance a tango during the next verse.)

GORDON.
BRAIN DEAD.
DRESSED UP AND WE'RE CHATTING

AND I'M BRAIN DEAD.
YOU DESERVE AN EXPLANATION.
BRAIN DEAD.
SITTING IN THIS RESTAURANT TONIGHT.

WAITER —
LATER.
PLEASE WE'RE TALKING.

ROGER.
I SAID:
"YOU HAVE LIMITATIONS, DARLING."

GORDON.
INSTEAD
SCREAM YOUR ACCUSATIONS.
DON'T BE WELL BRED
LIFE AIN'T ALWAYS HAPPINESS AND LIGHT.

I THOUGHT
IF I COULD FINISH
A SONG OR FIVE,
I'D BE BRAIN DEAD
BUT ALIVE.

(More tango. GORDON dances ROGER near to the wings. The DANCE changes into a Greek step dance with the entire cast following ROGER in a line, hands above their heads, stepping smartly.)

GORDON.
LAST SCENE:
EV'RYBODY'S DANCING.
I TAKE CODEINE.
LOVERS START ROMANCING.
THERE'S A BRIGHT GREEN
THING BETWEEN YOUR TEETH, DEAR.
PLEASE DON'T SMILE.

WAITER —
LATER,
PLEASE WE'RE FIGHTING.

CRASH! BANG!
AT THIS SPEED IT'S STIMULATING.
CRASH! BANG!
I'M OUT HERE HALLUCINATING.

GORDON.
CRASH! BANG!
ACTUALLY I'M GOING OUT IN STYLE.
THAT SAID:
PLEASE SOMEONE KILL ME
IF I SURVIVE,
'CAUSE I'M BRAIN DEAD
AND A

(RHODA sits on GORDON's lap like she's a puppet. He's a bad ventriloquist mouthing the words as RHODA sings along.)

WHENEVER I DREAM

RHODA.
WHENEVER I DREAM
I DREAM PORNOGRAPHICALLY EXPLICIT.
I DREAM I'M A HORSE,
WHICH IS PROB'LY A PENIS,
BUT IS IT?
IS IT?
I DON'T KNOW.
THINGS THAT I THINK MEAN ONE THING
SOMETIMES DO, SOMETIMES DON'T.
THE WORLD IS A CONFUSING PLACE TO LIVE IN.

BUT WHAT I MEAN IS
WE GET BY.
IN MY DREAMS I'M ALWAYS UP AND WALKING.
SELF-ASSURED, SELF-DECEIVED,
NOT ABOUT TO DIE.
BUT WHEN I WAKE IT'S GONE.
AND THEN I CARRY ON.
WHENEVER I DREAM,
I DON'T DREAM THAT I'M WRITING SOMETHING TAWDRY
I WRITE ABOUT HOW I'M A COW
THEN I BECOME MY COUSIN AUDRY.
TAWDRY?
GORDON.
YES IT IS.

RHODA.
THINGS THAT I THINK MEAN ONE THING

SOMETIMES DO, SOMETIMES DON'T.
THE WORLD IS: *(GORDON drinks some water and RHODA garbles the next line)*
CONFUSING PLACE TO LIVE IN.

BUT OUT THERE NO ONE UNDERSTANDS.
IN MY DREAMS I'M ALL COMPOSED, COMPOSING.
AT THE KEYS, SYMPHONIES
DRIP FROM THESE TWO HANDS;
BUT WHEN I WAKE IT'S GONE.
AND THEN I CARRY ON.

(This gradually get more spastic and out of control.)

WHENEVER I DREAM
WHENEVER I LAUGH
WHENEVER I SPRING
WHENEVER I EAT
WHENEVER I SPRING
WHENEVER I FART
WHENEVER I SPRING
WHENEVER I DREAM
WHENEVER I DREAM
WHENEVER I DREAM
WHENEVER I DREAM
YA YA YA YA YA YA YA

WHENEVER I DREAM
WHENEVER I LAUGH
WHENEVER I SPRING
WHENEVER I EAT
WHENEVER I SPRING

RHODA.
WHENEVER I FART
WHENEVER I SPRING
WHENEVER I DREAM
WHENEVER I DREAM
WHENEVER I DREAM
WHENEVER I DREAM
YA YA YA YA YA YA YA

EATING MYSELF UP ALIVE

(Sort of an Aretha with the Pips)

RICHARD.
I'M EATING MYSELF UP ALIVE.
LEARNING TO DRINK
BITING MY FINGER.
EAT EAT EAT EAT
EATING MYSELF UP ALIVE.

I'M EATING MYSELF UP ALIVE.
MEMORIES STINK
MEMORIES LINGER.
EAT EAT EAT EAT
EATING MYSELF UP ALIVE.

HOMELESS WOMAN, DOCTOR, MINISTER, NANCY D.

WHERE THE HELL'S MY SENSE OF HUMOR?
WHERE THE HELL'S MY DRIVE?
WATCHING TV
TOSSING IN BED
EATING MYSELF UP ALIVE.

OOH —
(Echo)
EATING MYSELF UP

TELL ME THE TRUTH —
WAS IT SOMETHING I SAID?
EATING AND EATING AND
EATING MYSELF UP ALIVE.

OH —

WO — OH —
OH —
OH —
EATING MYSELF UP ALIVE

EAT EAT EAT
EAT EAT EAT
EAT EAT EAT
EAT EAT EAT

WO — OH —
OH —
OH —
EATING MYSELF UP

EAT EAT EAT
EAT EAT EAT
EAT EAT EAT
EAT EAT
EATING MYSELF UP

IT'S AWFUL TO ALWAYS BE NICE

GORDON.
SOMETIMES I FAIL

RICHARD.
SOMETIMES IT'S STINKY
EAT EAT EAT EAT

EATING MYSELF UP ALIVE

I'M PAYING A HORRIBLE PRICE.
BITING THE NAIL
OFF OF MY PINKY.
EAT EAT EAT EAT
EATING MYSELF UP ALIVE.

IF I'VE LOST MY SENSE OF HUMOR	OOH —
HOW WILL I SURVIVE?	
GRINDING MY TEETH	
THROWING A FIT	
EATING MYSELF UP ALIVE.	
	EATING MYSELF UP
IS THERE A FOOD WE ADORE	
MORE THAN CHOCOLATE?	
EATING AND EATING AND	NOO —
EATING MYSELF UP ALIVE.	OOH —
	EAT EAT EAT
WO — OH —	EAT EAT EAT
OH —	EAT EAT EAT
OH —	EAT EAT EAT
EATING MYSELF UP ALIVE	
	EAT EAT EAT
WO — OH —	EAT EAT EAT
OH —	EAT EAT EAT
OH —	EAT EAT EAT

(Shouts) Spell it!

HOMELESS WOMAN, DOCTOR, MINISTER, NANCY D.
E-a-t-i-n-g
M-y-s-e-l-f
U-p
A-l-i-v-e

RICHARD.
ALIVE —

HOMELESS WOMAN, DOCTOR, MINISTER, NANCY D.
ALIVE!
E-a-t-i-n-g
M-y-s-e-l-f
U-p
A-l-i-v-e

RICHARD.
ALIVE —
HOMELESS WOMAN,
DOCTOR, MINISTER,
NANCY D.
ALIVE!

RICHARD, HW, DOCTOR, MINISTER, NANCY D.	**RHODA.**	**GORDON.**	**ROGER.**
	DREAM,	BRAIN DEAD.	BRAIN DEAD.
EATING MYSELF UP,	DREAM,		
EATING MYSELF UP,	DREAM,		
EATING MYSELF UP,	DREAM,	WHAT THE	BRAIN DEAD.
		HELL IS	
EATING MYSELF UP,	DREAM,	GOING ON?	
EATING MYSELF UP,	DREAM,		
EATING MYSELF UP,	YA YA YA YA	BRAIN DEAD.	BRAIN DEAD.
EATING MYSELF UP,	DREAM,		
EATING MYSELF UP,	DREAM,		
EATING MYSELF UP,	DREAM,		
EATING MYSELF UP,	DREAM,	I DON'T THINK I	BRAIN DEAD.
EATING MYSELF UP,	DREAM,	LIKE IT HERE.	
EATING MYSELF UP.	DREAM.	BRAIN DEAD.	BRAIN DEAD.

RICHARD.
EATING AND EATING AND
EATING AND EATING AND
EATING MYSELF UP ALIVE!

1-2-3– Spell it!

THE MUSIC STILL PLAYS ON

(A begowned MOTHER in a romantic concert sings.)

MOTHER.
I HAD A SON.
HE WAS ONE
OF A KIND.
SON-OF-A-GUN —
WE WERE TOO INTERTWINED.

I LOOK DAMN GOOD IN A HAT.
MY BLACK DRESS HIDES THE FAT.
I DON'T WANT SYMPATHY.
HE WAS HERE AND NOW HE'S GONE.
THE MUSIC STILL PLAYS ON.

(Looking at GORDON playing the piano.)

I SEE THE KEYS,
AND I FREEZE:
NO SURPRISE.
THIS IS HOW HE THINKS
I'LL BE
WHEN HE DIES.
I'LL BE GRACIOUS AND ALOOF;
OR I'LL CLIMB ON THE ROOF
SHOUTING OBSCENITIES.
HE WAS HERE AND NOW HE'S GONE,
THE MUSIC STILL PLAYS ON.

THE MUSIC STILL PLAYS ON AND ON AND ON AND ON
LOUD AND FAST AND CLEAR.
THE MUSIC STILL PLAYS ON AND ON AND ON AND ON
EVEN THOUGH YOU'RE NOT HERE,
MY DEAD.

MARRIED TOO YOUNG,
I WAS BRASH, I WAS BOLD.
MARRIED TOO YOUNG
AND DIVORCED FAR TOO OLD.

HUSBAND'S SLEEKER THAN A HORSE;
HE REARS AND FLIES OFF COURSE.
I LIKED HIS PEDIGREE.
LOVE IS HERE AND THEN IT'S GONE.
THE MUSIC STILL PLAYS ON.

THE MUSIC STILL PLAYS ON AND ON AND ON AND ON —
AS MY MEN DEPART.
THE MUSIC STILL PLAYS ON AND ON AND ON AND ON
TRANSMITTED THROUGH
MY FOO-
LISH HEART.

MOTHER.
SO STAY AWAY.
I'M OKAY,
I'M AHEAD.
WHAT CAME TO PASS —
ONE'S AN ASS
ONE IS DEAD.
LOVE IS STUPID AND IT BLEEDS.
IT SATISFIES MY NEEDS.
I THINK IT'S WONDERFUL.
ONCE IT WAS WONDERFUL.
LOVE IS HERE AND THEN IT'S GONE.
THE MUSIC STILL PLAYS ON.
THEY WERE HERE AND NOW THEY'RE GONE.
THE MUSIC STILL PLAYS ON AND ON AND ON.

DON'T GIVE IN

(MR. BUNGEE enters on his scooter. He turns to the audience.)

BUNGEE. Hey, there, little tadpoles. Kerplop! Aren't we having a fungee-bungee good time. Come on, let's hip hop over to my own little lily pad on this dark and miserable morning, at least it's dark and miserable here, and maybe it's dark where you are too. Uh-oh. Looks like somebody hasn't been listening to Mr. Bungee.

(BUNGEE has seen GORDON lying in his coma; BUNGEE sings to him.)

WHEN YOU WANT TO QUIT
'CAUSE NOTHING WORKS —
DON'T GIVE IN.
QUITTING IS THE SPECIALTY OF JERKS —
DON'T GIVE IN.
SIMPLY KEEP YOUR FOCUS
ON WHAT LIES AHEAD.
DON'T PLAY GAMES.
DON'T PLAY DEAD.
BEGIN.
THOSE WHO ARE MARKING TIME,
WAKE UP.
LIFE IS A CAUSE THAT YOU HAVE TO TAKE UP.
DO-O-O-N'T GIVE IN.

(GORDON wakes up and joins MR. BUNGEE who no longer seems toxic.)

BUNGEE.
WHEN YOU THINK YOU'RE DYING,
WELL YOU AIN'T.
ALL YOU NEED'S ANOTHER COAT OF PAINT.
DON'T GIVE IN.
FIX A-THIS AND FIX A-THAT
AND YOU'LL SURMISE
NO MORE ALIBIS
WHY YOU DID NOT WIN.
WHAT ONCE SEEMED BOORISH AND HOKEY
NOW SEEMS INCREDIBLY OKEY-DOKEY.
DO-O-O-O-N'T GIVE IN.

(Al Jolson-like) WHEN YOU'RE FEELING LOW.
GORDON.
WHEN I'M FEELING LOW?
BUNGEE.
MAYBE EAT SPAGHETTI.
GORDON.
SPAGHETTI.
BUNGEE.
JUST AS LONG AS YOU
CONTINUE ON
GORDON.
I LIKE SPAGHETTI.
BUNGEE.
EVERY DAY YOU'LL GROW.
YOU'LL BECOME MORE READY
TO CONFRONT THE DARK'
BEFORE THE DAWN.

(ROGER, MOTHER and RHODA wheel the bed in, focusing on GORDON in bed. Actually he's out of bed standing with MR. BUNGEE.)

BUNGEE.
WHEN YOU WANT TO QUIT
'CAUSE NOTHING WORKS —
ROGER, MOTHER, RHODA.
DON'T GIVE IN.
BUNGEE.
QUITTING IS THE SPECIALTY OF JERKS.

ROGER, MOTHER, RHODA.
DON'T GIVE IN.
BUNGEE.
SIMPLY KEEP YOUR FOCUS
ON WHAT LIES AHEAD
ROGER.
DON'T PLAY GAMES.
RHODA.
DON'T PLAY DEAD.
MOTHER.
BEGIN, DARLING. BEGIN.
BUNGEE.
THOSE WHO ARE MARKING TIME,
WAKE UP.
MOTHER.
WAKE UP.
RHODA.
WAKE UP.
ROGER.
WAKE UP.
BUNGEE and GORDON.
LIFE IS A CAUSE THAT YOU HAVE TO TAKE UP.

(GORDON lies down in the bed.)

ALL except GORDON.
DO-O-O-O-N'T GIVE IN!
GORDON. *(Waking up from the coma, mumbling at first)*
WHEN YOU WANT TO QUIT 'CAUSE NOTHING WORKS,
QUITTING IS THE SPECIALTY OF ...

(Everyone's thrilled and embracing.)

BUNGEE.
STRANGE THINGS HAPPEN MORE THAN YOU WOULD GUESS —
DON'T GIVE IN.
WHEN LIFE SEEMS AN UNFORGIVING MESS —
DON'T GIVE IN.
THINGS GO WRONG,
YOU LOOSE YOUR WAY,
BUT DON'T DESPAIR.
JUST PLAY FAIR AND PREPARE
TO WIN.
WHAT ONCE WAS WRONG IS SOON RIGHTED;

MIS'RABLE PEOPLE BECOMES DELIGHTED.
DON'T GIVE IN.

YOU BOYS ARE GONNA GET ME IN SUCH TROUBLE

RICHARD. Time for our last sponge bath together.
ROGER. He's gonna take a real shower.
RICHARD. It's only been two weeks.
ROGER. He's ready.
GORDON. I'm ready.
RICHARD. No no no.
ROGER. Yes yes yes.
RICHARD. No no no.
ROGER. Yes yes yes.
RICHARD.
YOU BOYS
ARE GONNA
GET ME
IN SUCH TROUBLE.
OH YOU BOYS
NAUGHTY BOYS.
RICHARD'S GONNA CATCH SOME HELL
FOR THIS.
RICHARD'S GONNA CATCH SOME HELL.

GORDON and RICHARD.
RICHARD'S GONNA CATCH SOME HELL FOR THIS.
RICHARD'S GONNA CATCH SOME HELL.

(They go to take their shower.)

RICHARD.
BUT I DON'T CARE.
NO I DON'T CARE.
A NURSE
SHOULD HELP A PATIENT GET BETTER.
NOT ALWAYS ACCORDING TO THE LETTER.
THAT'S WHY YOU BOYS ARE GETTING
WETTER AND WETTER.

YOU BOYS
ARE GONNA

RICHARD.
GET ME
IN SUCH TROUBLE.

OH YOU BOYS
NAUGHTY BOYS
RICHARD'S GONNA CATCH SOME HELL
FOR THIS.
RICHARD'S GONNA CATCH SOME HELL.

GORDON and RICHARD.
RICHARD'S GONNA CATCH SOME HELL FOR THIS.
RICHARD'S GONNA CATCH SOME HELL.

RICHARD.
ARE YOU ALL RIGHT IN THERE?
GORDON and RICHARD.
YES, WE'RE ALL RIGHT IN HERE!
RICHARD.
HAVE YOU GOT SOAP?
GORDON and RICHARD.
YEAH, WE GOT SOAP!
RICHARD.
AND SOME SHAMPOO?
GORDON and RICHARD.
YES, SIR, WE DO!
RICHARD.
ARE YOU ALL RIGHT IN THERE?
GORDON and RICHARD.
YES, WE'RE ALL RIGHT!

RICHARD.
RICHARD'S GONNA CATCH SOME HELL FOR THIS.
RICHARD'S GONNA CATCH SOME HELL FOR THIS.
RICHARD'S GONNA CATCH SOME HELL FOR THIS.
RICHARD'S GONNA CATCH
RICHARD'S GONNA CATCH
RICHARD'S GONNA CATCH SOME HELL.

GORDON. *(Showering.)*
I FELL LIKE I'M SAILING.
IT'S INSANE.
BUT I CHOOSE TO LIVE.
BEFORE WAS A FAILING

OF MY BRAIN
WHICH YOU MUST FORGIVE.
THE WATER HITS MY NECK;
THE WIND IS IN MY FACE.
ALL GONE IS INCREDIBLE STRIFE.
AND
I FEEL LIKE I'M SAILING
I'M SLOWLY EXHALING
HOLDING ON FOR LIFE.

HOMELESS LADY'S REVENGE

HOMELESS WOMAN. Books for sale! Two bucks a book! "The Selected Stories of Gertrude Stein" was originally eighteen bucks, my price — two bucks!
WE HAVE BOOKS.
ALL SORTS OF FICTION
YOU CAN BUY
AT A DISCOUNT.
AS OF THIS COUNT,
ONE HUNDRED AND THREE BOOKS —
FROM CLASSICS TO MYSTERY,
ALSO GAY HISTORY
HERE ON THE STREET.

WHERE DO I GET THEM?
I HAVE MY SOURCES.
READERS' DIVORCES.
LIVES GO BAD.
KIDS GO TO COLLEGE.
MOTHERS THROW THEIR BOOKS AWAY.
AND MOTHERS THROW THEIR BOOKS AWAY
WHEN MOTHERS GET MAD.

WE HAVE BOOKS.
HANDSOME BOOKS.
ALL THESE BOOKS DISPLAYED IN MY TROLLEY.
POEMS, PORNO, AND WHACKERY,
ALSO SOME THACKERAY
HERE
HERE
ON THE STREET.

(GORDON can be walking with a cane.)

GORDON.
FIRST DAY OUT.
ROGER.
JUST TO THE BANK AND BACK.
GORDON.
I FEEL ABOUT EIGHT.
ROGER.
DON'T HYPERVENTILATE.
IT'S NORMAL OUT ON THE STREET
INFORMAL, LOVELY, AND SWEET.
GORDON.
IT'S RAINING, WHICH I ABHOR.
ROGER.
BUT YOU WON'T FIND HIM COMPLAINING
ANYMORE.
GORDON.
NO, NO MORE.

HOMELESS WOMAN.
WE HAVE BOOKS.
GORDON and ROGER.
LIFE IS WONDERFUL
HOMELESS WOMAN.
FANCY BOOKS.
GORDON and ROGER.
VERY WONDERFUL.
HOMELESS WOMAN.
KIND OF DAMP BUT STILL QUITE LEGIBLE
JAMES BOND UP THROUGH DOCTOROW.
WORLD'S FAIR OR IT'S *DR. NO*
HERE HERE ON THE STREET.

GORDON.
I CAN'T BELIEVE WHAT I SEE
HALF THESE BOOKS BELONG TO ME.
HALF THESE BOOKS WITH MY NAME ON THE COVER.
ROGER.
SOME WITH THE NAME OF YOUR LOVER.
GORDON.
BUT YOU HAVE FOUND MY BOOKS.
YOU HAVE FOUND MY HISTORY.
OH, YOU DON'T KNOW WHAT THIS MEANS TO ME.
IT MEANS TO ME I LIVE. I LIVE.
But I want my books back.

(HOMELESS WOMAN holds up two fingers.)

GORDON. I'm not paying for my own goddamn books.

(ROGER tries to avoid a fight.)

ROGER.
LADY GRACE.
DO YOU RECOGNIZE MY FACE?
HOMELESS WOMAN.
TWO BUCKS.
ROGER.
IN AN INVITING PLACE
HOMELESS WOMAN.
TWO BUCKS.
ROGER.
I AM SOMEONE YOU HAVE COUNSELED ONCE BEFORE.
HOMELESS WOMAN.
DON'T TOUCH THEM.
ROGER. *(Trying to hand her money)*
BLINK OR SOMEHOW TRY TO SHOW
GORDON. Roger.
ROGER.
I AM SOMEONE WHO YOU KNOW.
GORDON. You're not paying —
ROGER.
PLEASE FORGIVE ME IF I STAND HERE TO IMPLORE.
BUT HERE'S HIS WHOLE LIBRARY,
WHICH I THINK VERY VERY
WELL WORTH FIGHTING FOR!

HOMELESS WOMAN.
I DON'T CARE IF YOU'RE THE KING
OF ENGLAND.
I DON'T CARE IF YOU'RE A SAINT.
IT'S TWO BUCKS.
I DON'T CARE IF LIFE'S A SILLY
PICNIC,
WHICH IS SOMETHING THAT IT AIN'T.
IT'S TWO BUCKS.
TWO BUCKS IF YOU WERE MY
MOTHER.
TWO BUCKS IF YOU WERE MY DOG.

GORDON.
What?

I really hate crazy
people.

ROGER.	**GORDON.**	**HOMELESS WOMAN.**
	WHERE DID YOU FIND	
YOU'RE MAKING HIM	THEM?	I HAVE MY
CRAZY.		SOURCES.
	YOU'RE MAKING ME	READER'S
OH, JESUS	CRAZY.	DIVORCES
CHRIST		LIVES GO BAD.

GORDON.
BUT THESE ARE MINE.
HOMELESS WOMAN.
NOT ANYMORE, THEY AREN'T.
MOTHERS THROW THESE BOOKS SWAY.
GORDON.
BUT THESE ARE MINE.
HOMELESS WOMAN.
MOTHERS THROW THEIR BOOKS SWAY
WHEN MOTHERS GET MAD.
COME BUY THEM . . .
COME BUY THEM.

TIME

ROGER. What are you doing, Gordo? They're only books.
GORDON. What am I doing?
EVERYTHING HAS CHANGED AND NOTHING'S CHANGED.
What am I doing?
I MEAN, I'M DIFFERENT, BUT I'M STILL THE SAME.
I STILL COMPLAIN.
BUT I'M NOT THE SAME THAT I WAS,
EXCEPT I'M THE SAME THAT I WAS.
BUT DIFFERENT.
AS LEAST I HOPE I'M DIFFERENT.

SO ON THIS NEW DAY,
LET'S BEGIN FROM SCRATCH.

ROGER.
THE PLEASURE'S MINE.
I GIVE YOU TIME.
I GIVE YOU TIME TO SCREW AROUND.
I GIVE YOU TIME TO KISS THE GROUND.
I GIVE YOU TIME.
I GIVE YOU TIME TO VALUE WHAT YOU'VE FOUND.

AND MOST OF ALL, MY FRIEND,
I GIVE YOU TIME.

MINISTER.
STORIES OF MOTHERS
STORIES OF BOYFRIENDS
AND TALES OF HOW ROMANCE SURVIVES.
STORIES OF LIVING
OF ALMOST FORGIVING
AND POOR, UNSUCCESSFUL, AND FAT PEOPLE'S LIVES.

GORDON.
BUT YA GOTTA HAVE TIME AND MUSIC
YA GOTTA HAVE TIME AND MUSIC.

GORDON and ROGER.
TIME AND MUSIC GET ALONG.

DOCTOR, ROGER, GORDON, MOTHER, RICHARD.	**RHODA, HOMELESS WOMAN, NANCY D., MINISTER.**
	YA GOTTA HAVE TIME
YOU GOTTA HAVE	AND MUSIC.
TIME AND MUSIC	TIME —
YA GOTTA HAVE	
TIME AND MUSIC	TIME AND MUSIC
TIME AND MUSIC MAKE	TIME AND MUSIC MAKE
A SONG	A SONG
OH YA GOTTA HAVE	OH YA GOTTA HAVE

ROGER. RICHARD.	**GORDON MOHTER.**	**HW, DOCOTR MINISTER.**	**RHODA NANCY D.**
TIME	TIME	TIME	TIME
EV'RYBODY	AND MUSIC	TIME AND MUSIC	YOU GOTTA HAVE TIME
GOTTA HAVE	YA GOTTA HAVE		
TIME AND MUSIC	TIME AND MUSIC	TIME AND MUSIC	YA GOTTA HAVE
TIME AND			
MUSIC	TIME AND MUSIC	YA GOTTA HAVE	TIME
OR YOU'RE NEVER	GET ALONG	SOME TIME	
GONNA GET ALONG		AND MUSIC	YOU'LL ALWAYS GET
NO NO NO NO NO	OH YA GOTTA HAVE	YEAH YEAH YEAH	ALONG WIIH YOUR
HAVE			TIME AND MUSIC
TIME EV'RYBODY	TIME AND MUSIC	TIME AND MUSIC	TIME
GOTTA HAVE	YA GOTTA HAVE	TIME AND MUSIC	YA GOTTA HAVE TIME
TIME AND MUSIC	TIME AND MUSIC		

GORDON.
TIME AND MUSIC MAKE
ALL.
TIME AND MUSIC MAKE
TIME AND MUSIC MAKE
GORDON.
MAKE A SONG
BUNGEE.
MAKE A SONG
HOMELESS WOMAN.
MAKE A SONG.

(Segue: "I FEEL LIKE SPRING.")

I FEEL SO MUCH SPRING

(GORDON is at the piano playing a new version of the first song.)

GORDON.
I FELL SO MUCH SPRING WITHIN ME.
BLOW, WINDS, BLOW;
SPRING HAS JUST BEGUN.
AND SOMETHING'S TAKEN WING WITHIN ME.
WHAT WAS DARK SO LONG
HAD FELT LIKE WINTER.
FINALLY THERE'S SUN;
AND SO I SING
THAT I FEEL SO MUCH SPRING.

HOMELESS WOMAN.
I FEEL SO MUCH DAWN AROUND ME.
SUN COMES UP,
ROTTEN TIMES HAVE BEEN AND GONE.
AND DAWN IS MUCH AROUND ME.
BIRDS ARE WHISTLING FOR THEIR CRAZY MAMA.
FLOWERS JOIN IN SONG —
I HEAR THEM SING;
AND I FEEL SO MUCH SPRING.

HOMELESS WOMAN and MINISTER.
IN THIS MOOD
I HEAR MUSIC, I DANCE NUDE

AND WON'T CLOSE THE BLIND

RHODA and NANCY D.

I THINK I'M FINALLY
LOSING MY MIND.

AH

AH
AH
AH
AH
AH

RHODA, HOMELESS WOMAN, NANCY D.

AND I FEEL SO MUCH SPRING
WITHIN ME.
BLOW WIND BLOW SPRING
HAS JUST BEGUN.

RICHARD.

AND I FEEL SO MUCH SPRING
WITHIN ME.
BLOW

HOMELESS WOMAN.

BLOW WIND BLOW SPRING HAS JUST BEGUN.

RHODA, NANCY D., HOMELESS WOMAN, DOCTOR, MINISTER, RICHARD, MOTHER.

AND SOMETHING'S TAKEN WING WITHIN ME.
WHAT WAS DEAD SO LONG
HAD FELT LIKE WINTER;
FINALLY THERE'S SUN!

ALL.

THERE'S SUN!

I FEEL SO MUCH SPRING WITHIN ME.
BLOW, WINDS, BLOW.
SPRING HAS JUST BEGUN.
AND SOMETHING'S TAKEN WING WITHIN ME.

GORDON.

WHAT WAS DARK SO LONG
HAD FELT LIKE WINTER.
FINALLY, THERE'S SUN!
AND SO I SING
THAT I FEEL SO MUCH SPRING.

NANCY D.

I FEEL SO MUCH SPRING.

ROGER.
I FEEL SO MUCH SPRING.
HOMELESS WOMAN.
I FEEL SO MUCH SPRING.
MINISTER.
I FEEL SO MUCH SPRING.
RHODA.
I FEEL SO MUCH SPRING.
DOCTOR.
I FEEL SO MUCH SPRING.
RICHARD.
I FEEL SO MUCH SPRING.
MR. BUNGEE.
TIME AND MUSIC.
GORDON.
I FEEL SO MUCH SPRING.
MOTHER.
TIME AND MUSIC.
GORDON.
I FEEL SO MUCH SPRING.
OTHERS.
TIME AND MUSIC.
GORDON. *(Perfectly content)*
I FEEL SO MUCH SPRING.

THE END

OTHER TITLES AVAILABLE FROM SAMUEL FRENCH

THE MUSICAL OF MUSICALS (THE MUSICAL!)

Music by Eric Rockwell
Lyrics by Joanne Bogart
Book by Eric Rockwell and Joanne Bogart

2m, 2f / Musical / Unit Set

The Musical of Musicals (The Musical!) is a musical about musicals! In this hilarious satire of musical theatre, one story becomes five delightful musicals, each written in the distinctive style of a different master of the form, from Rodgers and Hammerstein to Stephen Sondheim. The basic plot: June is an ingenue who can't pay the rent and is threatened by her evil landlord. Will the handsome leading man come to the rescue? The variations are: a Rodgers & Hammerstein version, set in Kansas in August, complete with a dream ballet; a Sondheim version, featuring the landlord as a tortured artistic genius who slashes the throats of his tenants in revenge for not appreciating his work; a Jerry Herman version, as a splashy star vehicle; an Andrew Lloyd Webber version, a rock musical with themes borrowed from Puccini; and a Kander & Ebb version, set in a speakeasy in Chicago. This comic valentine to musical theatre was the longest running show in the York Theatre Company's 35-year history before moving to Off-Broadway.

"Witty! Refreshing! Juicily! Merciless!"
- Michael Feingold, *Village Voice*

"A GIFT FROM THE MUSICAL THEATRE GODS!"
– *TalkinBroadway.com*

"Real Wit, Real Charm! Two Smart Writers and Four Winning Performers! You get the picture, it's GREAT FUN!"
- *The New York Times*

"Funny, charming and refreshing!
It hits its targets with sophisticated affection!"
- *New York Magazine*

SAMUELFRENCH.COM

OTHER TITLES AVAILABLE FROM SAMUEL FRENCH

SHINE!
THE HORATIO ALGER MUSICAL

Book by Richard Seff
Music by Roger Anderson
Lyrics by Lee Goldsmith

All Groups / Musical / 13m, 6f / Various Sets

This charming rags to riches romp with a melodic score follows Ragged Dick, Horatio Alger's first best selling hero, from penniless bootblack to budding Wall Street entrepreneur. His adventures bring him face to face with scheming ex convicts, vicious comic villians, kind benefactors and a world of colorful street characters. Set in the New York Centennial summer of 1876, this full of hopes and dreams musical is perfect for the whole family. Winner of the National Music Theatre Network Award.

"Highly tuneful.... A friendly show of considerable good humor."
- *Playbill on Line*

OTHER TITLES AVAILABLE FROM SAMUEL FRENCH

ADRIFT IN MACAO

Book and Lyrics by Christopher Durang
Music by Peter Melnick

Full Length / Musical / 4m, 3f / Unit Sets

Set in 1952 in Macao, China, *Adrift In Macao* is a loving parody of film noir movies. Everyone that comes to Macao is waiting for something, and though none of them know exactly what that is, they hang around to find out. The characters include your film noir standards, like Laureena, the curvacious blonde, who luckily bumps into Rick Shaw, the cynical surf and turf casino owner her first night in town. She ends up getting a job singing in his night club – perhaps for no reason other than the fact that she looks great in a slinky dress. And don't forget about Mitch, the American who has just been framed for murder by the mysterious villain McGuffin. With songs and quips, puns and farcical shenanigans, this musical parody is bound to please audiences of all ages.